Woman on the Wire

An Ellen Parker Novel

Woman on the Wire

An Ellen Parker Novel

Steven M. Silver

Dedication

Carmesha Rogers
"Just get the kids out of the way. 'Cause I'd want someone to do that for my kids."

Antoinette Tuff
"But, look at me now. I'm still working and everything is OK."

Malala Yousafzai
"This is the forgiveness that I have learned from my father and from my mother. This is what my soul is telling me. Be peaceful and love everyone."

Acknowledgments

Once again, thanks to Eric for his cover, proof reading, and encouragement. And thanks for Jeanie for herself.

Given my background as a psychotherapist who has spent most of his adult life working with veterans recovering from war trauma, it may be tempting for someone to try to match some of the characters here with some of those veterans. Don't. All of these people are, for better or worse, figments of my imagination. Nonetheless, from 1972 to the present day, that work has acquainted me with some people best described as magnificent and I hope the portrayals I've made will be taken by them as both accurate and respectful. I deeply appreciate their willingness to share with me their experiences and I hope I have made some contribution to their coming home.

Military sexual trauma, referred to here, is unfortunately common. An Department of Defense report cited by the Public Broadcasting System, http://www.pbs.org/now/shows/336/fact-check-military-sexual-trauma.html, provides statistics for those seeking them.

The move of prison gangs into the mainstream is also common. (See http://www.fbi.gov/stats-services/publications/2011-national-gang-threat-assessment for an introduction to this growing problem). The problem, described earlier in the first Ellen Parker novel, *A Dangerous Man,* has, if anything, gotten worse, with prison gangs, such as the 211 Crew, suspected in the killings of public prosecutors and the head of the Dept. of Corrections for Colorado.

There is, at this writing, a Philly.com (http://www.philly.com/), a partner to the Philadelphia Inquirer and the Philadelphia Daily News. I have taken enormous liberties with how Philly.com works for the sake of the story but have tried to color within the lines.

All data cited in this novel, particularly that pertaining to the work of the FBI and other law enforcement agencies is taken from their respective reports. I've been lucky enough to know officers and agents over the years and hope that, as with the two previous Ellen Parker novels, they find my portrayals of their fictional equivalents reasonable.

Chester County, Pennsylvania
Spring, 2013

Day One

Chapter 1

"She's been dead not much more than twelve hours," the medical examiner said. He had a blue windbreaker on over his brown suit; the tall, yellow "ME" on his back was as crisp and sharp as the early morning air. Still squatting beside the corpse, he turned to the two police officers standing behind him and pushed his glasses up on his nose with a latex-gloved pinky.

"She wasn't killed here," he said. "Lividity, what I can see so far, lack of blood around her, and her wrists," he nodded to one side, "all say she was dead before she was tied to the fence."

The woman leaned into the ancient barbed wire. Her arms were outstretched, her wrists bound to the upper strand with stiff wire folded over on itself. Her head slumped forward, her long blond hair straggling down. Several obvious stab wounds marked her breasts and dried blood from them covered her torso down to her reddish-blond pubic hair.

"Cause of death?" The tall cop, a black man with gray at his temples, was in civilian clothes. The white man next to him was in the uniform of a Pennsylvania State Trooper and wore his broad brimmed hat pulled low, shadowing his pink face from the morning light.

"Need to look," the M.E. said. He stood, brushing his gloved hands together. "The stabbing might have done it but it looks like she took some hits to the skull that were pretty severe." He shook his head.

"Yeah," the cop said to the M.E.'s unspoken words. "Nasty."

"She didn't go peaceably," the M.E. said. He stepped to one of her hands and pointed. "It looks like she hit something with her knuckles." He looked at the cop. "I think there's material under the fingernails of the other hand. Bruise on the top of her right foot. Maybe from the perpetrator, maybe from kicking someone."

"The top of the foot?" the trooper asked. He frowned as he considered the comment.

1

"A lot of kicks impact in that fashion," the M.E. said. He took plastic bags from his jacket's pockets and put one around her hand. "Some martial arts teach kicking like that."

"The marks on the inner thighs, those are post mortem," he said. "Some kind of design. Drawn, not slashed. He wasn't in a rage when he did those."

The black cop squatted to see better.

"Yeah," he said, examining the cuts. His gloved hands touched nothing but he held a finger close to the cuts, measuring their dimensions. They were small, no more than a couple of inches in length. They had not bled. They looked a little like stylized lightning marks, a pair close together on each thigh.

"Advertising," he said. The M.E. raised an eyebrow but the black cop added nothing. He stood, his eyes still on the cuts.

"The forensic services unit people are on their way," the black cop said to the white one. "Remind them not to cut the wire around her wrists." As the trooper nodded, he added. "I don't suppose they will but it won't hurt to say it." He looked up at several people at the side of the road standing next to a green tractor. "Is that the man who found her?"

"Yes, sir," the trooper said. A small notepad appeared almost magically in his hands. "Carl Tailor. Trooper Johnson is with him. Owns this patch of woods and the land on both sides of the road all the way down into that hollow." He motioned with his chin. "He said he was cutting the weeds along the shoulder and saw her hair."

"Good eyes. Has to be twenty yards from here to where his tractor is stopped."

"The fence parallels the road before it turns in here but remains about fifteen feet from the shoulder the whole side of the woods." The trooper looked up. "He says this is one of the few places where it is up and intact, that it's twenty or thirty years old. The wood lot grew up around it."

"Someone pulled off the road, carried her into the woods, and wired her up to the barbed wire. Twelve or so hours ago it was dark." He looked down the road. "I can't see his house."

"Down in the hollow. The road climbs back up and goes behind the far hill. Next house is a quarter of a mile beyond at the end of a lane."

"He see anything before spotting her?"

"Says not. Watched the Phillies lose. Wife went to bed at ten, game was over a little after eleven. He didn't notice any traffic."

"They get any?"

2

"Usually not," the trooper said. "That farm I mentioned, he says they would go in the other direction to pick up U.S. 30 to get anywhere. Occasionally kids drive by, looking for a deserted place to make out." He pointed. "At the edge of the lot, there's a dirt track between the wood lot and the corn field. Once or twice a year a kid will park there. He said he found a bunch of empty beer cans there last fall but nothing since."

"All right. I'll talk to him." He looked around; the scene was too ugly for the morning light. "Tell everyone to keep things sharp." He nodded to the medical examiner. "Doc, we're going to have visitors."

"The federal variety?"

"Yes."

"This has happened before." The ME wasn't asking a question.

"'Fraid so. About six weeks ago here in Pennsylvania, and Maryland, last year. Maybe other ones. There's a task force with the Fee-Bees, they'll be taking over, so let's keep it sharp."

"I always do."

"Of course." Doctors were always a little sensitive. He turned back to the uniformed trooper. "We'll walk the track and a broad front sweep from here to the road and to the track." He looked at the dead woman. She had once been pretty but murder and wounds had taken it all away. "Maybe we can find some trace of the son of a bitch who did this."

Chapter 2

On the other side of county, as emergency lights flashed silently near the body of a woman on an old wire fence, four men rode inside a black Chevrolet SUV and thought about their morning's chore. Robert Jacks – only a rare handful called him Bobby – closely studied the land around him with the intensity of a man looking for hope.

Given his occupation, some might have found this odd but everyone hopes and Bobby Jacks was living proof that people hope for the damnedest things.

Spring had come reluctantly to eastern Pennsylvania; the gray, cold misery of winter had held on like a dead hand in full rigor. But even the dead let go eventually, Jacks thought as he stared out the window of the big SUV. Green seemed to show in reluctant spots among the dead brown of the wooded lots they passed, but it showed.

He nodded. He liked spring. More exactly, he hated winter. Bobby Jacks glanced behind him at the men in the back seats. The one on the left, the young one, had his pistol in his lap. Jacks shook his head.

"You want to point that thing at the floor?"

"Sorry, Bobby."

"Mister Jacks – Tallman calls me Bobby. You don't."

"Got it, Mister Jacks."

"There it is, up ahead." The driver nodded as he spoke and Jacks turned to the front.

The trailer park was nothing much to look at. Someone had given up on grounds keeping a couple of years back and the blackberry bushes, their thin, reddish-brown arcs marking their territory, looked to make a fight of it if anything else tried to grow around them. The white fence bordering the road was missing pickets, drawing the eye to what wasn't there. Beyond them, the house trailers seemed few and some looked like they had been abandoned.

Maybe business would pick up when summer showed up, maybe not. Jacks thought not, though the large lake beyond the trailers might be an invitation to people looking for fishing or whatever the hell people did around lakes.

"All this place needs is tumbleweeds and crickets," the older man in the back seat said. Jacks agreed but he didn't show it; Jonesy, as the man was known, was an asshole. It was not Jack's idea to bring him along with the younger one. But Mr. Tallman wanted to give both a tryout and so here they were.

The black SUV turned into the entrance slowly. The place seemed deserted. Few of the trailers had a car near them. There were more empty slots than Jacks had thought there were. He shook his head again; Jonesy was right about tumbleweed rolling through it.

Sure, these "mom and pop" meth operations were everywhere and it made sense to keep them organized and under control so they didn't interfere with Mr. Tallman's operation. Yes, they were handy to take up the slack if there was a problem in the supply chain and there was money to be made moving their product. On the other hand, Mr. Tallman used industrial-sized supplies of ephedrine from India and Mexico and didn't mess with any over-the-counter bullshit, leaving that to the small producers he controlled.

But Jacks thought the small operators were more trouble than they were worth. They were disorganized, unreliable, and had a tendency to try to cheat. Case in point. He glanced at the driver as he scanned the area, looking for anything that might be trouble.

"Which one?"

"The white one," the driver said. He was the only one who had ever been here before, delivering and picking up. "The one with the, what you call it, garden shed behind it. Got the gray car parked beside it."

"OK, pull over here for a minute."

"Yes sir."

"Anyone see anything going on with any of the other trailers?"

"No."

"I got nothin'."

"Me, neither."

"Here's how we're going to do it, just like I told you before we left. We're going to pull in behind their car, it's on the far side. Leave the keys."

"Yes sir." That was the young one again. He was called Books but Jacks didn't know if that was his real name or some kind of nickname. Jacks figured he was trying to make an impression.

"Don't interrupt. They make the crystal in the shed." He looked at the driver, who nodded in confirmation. "Driver stays with our car in case they

5

try to come out a window. You two follow me. I go to the shed. You keep going to the door and go in. Get them down, put two in their heads, two each. Everyone, keep your guns out of sight except in the trailer or if they come out. Don't cowboy it. Get them down, then the head. Don't spray. Fucking rounds will go through that thing. It's just aluminum. We know the cash and product are in the shed – I'll get it. They keep the money in a blue backpack but the product may be bagged or loose, so be ready to lend a hand in gathering it up. We all go into the trailer to help look for the money if I don't find it immediately. Any questions?"

"No."

"Got it, Mister Jacks." Young guy again. At least he seemed to learn his manners.

"They have a kid." The driver rubbed his upper lip.

"So? If the kid is there, do it. Kid I.D.s you, you go down. Besides, part of this is to send people a message that Tallman is serious." Jacks paused. Of the three, the driver, in his opinion, had the most reliable credentials – everything he had said about the place had been true so far and he had never worked with the other two before, though Tallman seemed to think they were all right. He threw the driver a bone. "Thing is, we're coming at ten in the morning; kid's in school, right? Probably won't be there."

"Not a problem, just askin'."

"Any other questions? No? Ok, go ahead and pull around to the other side. Yeah, that's it, nice and easy. Middle of the day, just someone visiting. Guns out of sight. This is good. Stop here. Keep your eyes open. You two, out. Let's go."

"I see a car, babe." His voice was thin, tired, but she was used to hearing it that way and no longer noticed.

"We're in a fuckin' trailer park. Everyone's got a…"

"They're coming here."

"Let me see. Shit. Sharon! Sharon! Take out the ear things. Come on, just like we practiced." She half-dragged the little girl forward as if getting to the television that no longer worked was important.

"Not again. Davy, do I have to?"

"Do what she says, Sherrie. Hurry!"

"This is stupid." Her mother did not hear her. She grabbed a blue backpack and shoved it into the girl's hands, though it was a little large for a child.

6

"Hurry up. Here's your stuff. Good. Remember, whatever, you stay still until…"

"Until you open the trap door. This is stupid."

"Down. Down you go." Then the woman's desperation spoke. "I love you."

"All right, all right."

"Put it down, get the rug back."

"Got it, babe, got it. Where's my .45?"

"Here's one."

"Fuck. I don't like the Glock. Where's the shotgun?"

"By the bed, hurry!"

Books, the one who called Mister Jacks "Bobby," felt like he needed to get everything right so Mister Jacks would see that he was cool and not some cowboy. A professional, someone reliable. And maybe get a better nickname than "Books," which wasn't really a nickname, just his last name.

You look for your chances in life, your opportunities to get ahead. That's what this was for Books, an opportunity. He regarded himself only occupying a step above that of "entry level" – he had read an article about employment and the phrase had stuck with him. To get into "middle management" – same article – he was going to have to show something to the real decision makers in his organization, and Tallman and Jacks were not easily impressed.

Sure, dealing with a low-level manufacturer was a small assignment but it meant working with Mister Jacks, and Jacks had a very serious reputation. Books figured that this was one of those opportunities the article had talked about.

All it would take was two in the head.

He walked to the small stairs at the base of the trailer's entrance. He noticed that Jonesy walked well behind him, as if reluctant. Well, that was his problem. If he wanted to look reluctant, that was fine; it would make Books look better.

"Stay close," Books said over his shoulder. Jonesy said nothing but looked irritated; Books didn't know him very well but his reputation was he did not like taking orders. On the other hand, he was supposed to have killed someone a few months back, and that made him a potential rival for advancement.

Books stood with one foot on the top step, his hand on the butt of an automatic pistol resting in the small of his back. Mister Jacks already was at the large garden shed, a small pry bar in his hand. Jacks looked at the shed's padlock and then turned around and made eye contact.

He nodded to go ahead. Books nodded back, glanced at Jonesy standing behind him, and reached for the door handle.

Trying to turn the handle triggered four quick shots from inside the trailer, all of which were just over Books' head, tearing through the thin aluminum and leaving neat, uniform holes. Terrified, he dropped to the ground, his reflexes working even as the first bullet came. Jonesy crouched and pulled his pistol out of his jacket. He fired into the door, emptying the gun's fifteen rounds in a few seconds and squeezing even after the gun was emptied.

"Shit!" Books now was terrified of Jonesy, thinking the man had closed his eyes while he fired. He rolled to one side and then got to one knee. He pointed his own gun at the door just as Jacks arrived. Jacks impatiently held up his hand at him and then, standing to one side, tried the door.

The door swung open, revealing an interior too dark to see anything well. Books strained to see without standing but, other than the edge of a chair, he saw nothing worth shooting at. Jacks glanced at him and Jonesy and then snapped his head around the corner of the doorframe and then jerked it back. Drawing his pistol, he paused for a second, thinking.

Jacks, holding his gun with both hands, jumped into the trailer, just hitting the top step. Books scrambled to follow.

A woman, thin, stringy hair, lay on the carpet, her legs moving idly while her hands – they seemed almost like chicken feet they were so thin – pulled weakly at her bloody t-shirt; some of Jonesy's wild rounds had done some good. The t-shirt was something about Hawk Mountain, which Books had heard of, and looked like it was dirty before she got shot.

Books saw Jacks ignored her except to kick her pistol further away. Still holding his pistol out in front of him with both hands, he looked towards the front of the trailer but there was little to see except an old television and a filthy couch that Books didn't think he would sit on even if offered money. He turned with Jacks and faced the back.

Beyond a simple kitchen where dirty dishes seemed to be breeding with each other, a hallway formed by what was probably the bathroom ended in a cheap door marking the bedroom. He guessed the man was back there and copied Jacks' stance, moving to one side.

As he raised his pistol, the man appeared in the bedroom doorway. He had a shotgun leveled and Books thought for the third time he was about to be killed. Instinctively he fired and knew immediately he missed.

Jacks, though, did not miss. His shot, incredibly loud in the trailer, caused the man to flinch, folding into himself as if he had been punched. Jacks fired once more and the man convulsed, dropping the shotgun, and fell backwards, bouncing off the bed before landing on the floor.

Jacks walked forward, still holding his gun with both hands. He stood over the man and fired twice more. Then he looked back at Books.

"Finish her," he said, his voice seeming to come from very far away. Books looked down.

The woman still moved, though only slightly. Blood soaked into the ratty carpet. Books lowered his gun and pointed at her face. The woman did not see him. She mouthed words he could not hear. Then she seemed to gather herself.

"Run, Sherrie," she said. Her voice came from very far away. "Run."

Even as Books wondered if he could really do it, his finger squeezed. The nine-millimeter pistol barely bucked in his hand and a black dot about the size of the tip of his little finger appeared below her right eye. Her hands dropped away. The second shot, this one went into her temple, was so easy he smiled and considered a third until he remembered Jacks' instructions back in the car.

Two in the head.

Jacks moved quickly but controlled, like a dancer who knew exactly where a foot was going to be before it started to move. Books followed him back to the garden shed and Jacks had the pry bar in his hand before they reached the door.

The shed was big enough that it could have held a couple of riding mowers but that's not what was in it. A table on which glass jars, plastic jugs, and other paraphernalia used in the making of methamphetamine took up most of the space. Jacks ignored nearly all of it, his hands reaching for a pile of thick, plastic kitchen self-sealing bags, crammed with white powder.

"Pick up all of these," he said to Books and turned to meet the driver who came running around the corner. "What's the problem?"

"I think I saw the kid," the man said, gasping a little. "She's headed to the lake."

"Show me," Jacks said. He looked at Books. "All of the bags."

It took Books only a moment to scoop up all the bags – they were a little unwieldy but he made it to the SUV without the disaster of dropping one. He looked up as Jacks and the driver jogged back to them.

"All right," Jacks said and everyone leaned towards him; Books admired his ability to hold everyone's attention like that. That's how he wanted to be.

"The money's gone," Jacks said. "The backpack is missing. The kid may have it. And she may have seen us, so we've got to get her. She's got to be going around the lake in that direction," he waved his hand to one side. "You two," he nodded at Books and Jonesy, "are going to chase her. We know she went that way because there's brush and shit that she could hide in; the other way is wide open and we can't see her. While you go after her, we're going to take the car and circle around the other way. We'll get to the other side of the lake and then we'll have her between us." He paused.

"Here's the thing. She may have the money in a blue backpack. Driver says they kept the cash in one and thinks he saw it on her. Even if she doesn't, she has to go down. Most of the houses around the lake are empty this time of year he says," nodding at the driver, "just like the few trailers here. But don't be stupid. Stay close to the lake. People be less likely to see you. Keep moving, don't give her a chance to stop and think. Got it?"

Everyone nodded. Books looked at Jonesy.

"Let's go," he said, not waiting for Jacks to tell him to move. He jogged towards the lake, crossing over an empty trailer pad, and then turned in the direction they thought the girl had gone. The way ahead looked like heavy forest. It didn't matter. Jacks would circle around and they would find her.

And then it would be time for two in the head. He smiled.

Chapter 3

Jim Jeffers stood on the wooden deck tacked onto the back of the three-story, 150-year old building he owned and stretched. He grinned at himself when he heard popping in his shoulders and sat down on a folding chair. He reached down beside him and opened a large cooler and retrieved a can of diet soda. His hand grazed a bottle of beer but did not hesitate.

One day at a time.

He popped the can, took a sip, and grimaced.

"Tastes like shit," he said aloud.

"The wages of sin," a black woman's voice said, coming from the open door to the interior of the building. She finished strapping on a large wristwatch as she came into the morning sunlight. "If you weren't such an exploitive white landlord, you wouldn't be punished by having your taste buds cursed."

"Hey, breakfast of champions," he said.

She was shorter than his six feet, wore her hair cropped close while his dark hair dangled over his ears, and had a barely noticeable nub of a nose while he sported one that reminded more than one viewer of a classic American Indian. Her name was Aretha Taylor.

"What's new in the exciting world of social work?" Jeffers asked. He propped his feet up on a spare chair.

"Not a damned thing," Taylor said. She opened the cooler and took out one of the bottles of fruit juice; he packed them for her. In the late afternoon, the professor on the third floor brought wine when he came, which was seldom, and the remaining tenant, a veterinary student who was around even less than the professor, actually liked diet soda.

"The VA wants us to do more with less," she said, twisting the cap off and taking a good pull on the bottle. "Massa says don't work harder, work smarter. Assholes."

She pulled a chair next to his and sat down, glancing at her watch. She worked in a VA hospital twenty minutes away and was never late.

He let Taylor sit for a moment. Sometimes after a long week – sometimes after a long day – of wrestling with government bureaucracy, she needed to vent. Occasionally, when things were really a pain, she vented even before going to work. After a moment, she made a small smile and took a small drink of her juice.

"So?" he asked.

"So what?"

"Did you two talk?" He raised an eyebrow fairly successfully; he had had to practice the gesture.

"Couldn't reach her," Taylor said.

"Oh."

"Don't 'oh' me." She took a swallow. "I called three times and left messages." She looked down the hill. Below the house, fields rolled across the hills and merged into the gathering green of spring. "You know," Taylor said almost to herself, "we have a joke we tell about lesbian relationships."

"Probably nicer than the ones I know."

"What does a lesbian bring to her second date?"

"I don't know."

"A 'U-Haul.'"

"You two are long beyond the second date."

"Oh, yes, we are." She smiled slightly.

"So…" He sipped from his can. It did not taste any better.

"So, no, I'm not going to let a little spat mess us up. I'll get a hold of her…"

"Can I watch?"

"No, you pervert." Taylor grinned. "What I wanted to say is, I'll get a hold of her and get it straightened out." She shrugged. "Probably all my fault anyway."

"I'll drink to that." He listed his can and grinned. "I'm automatically on her side. I've always liked blonds. Especially blonds taking karate lessons." He raised his eyebrows. "The last time she was here, she seemed pretty clear about how she felt about you."

"Hey, are you giving relationship advice?" Taylor shook her head. "I'm a trained family therapist and your track record with relationships is dubious."

"Ouch. At least I'm sitting in the sun with a beautiful woman. Can't say the same for you."

"Stop, you'll turn my head. Have you heard from Karen?"

"Not since the last time you asked." Jeffers paused. "I only get the answering machine." It was his turn to shrug. "Maybe they're keeping her busy down there at Quantico."

"Maybe."

"Instructor and all. Not a lot of women instructors in the FBI, even nowadays."

"True."

"I think I told you, last time we talked she said her tour was almost over and she was thinking about putting in for the Philly field office."

"I remember."

"She didn't use the 'D' word." He grimaced. "So far I'm still one for two."

"Could be a good sign." Taylor nodded.

"She was still pissed that I wasn't lawyering."

"Might get used to that, given time and desire."

"Thinks being a landlord is beneath me."

"She say it like that?"

"No." Jeffers went silent for a moment. Taylor sipped her juice and waited. He could be quiet, especially when he was studying something.

"I think that might not be true," he said finally. "The drinking, yeah, there was no doubt that she thought *that* was beneath me. She doesn't understand why I left my job."

"Do you?"

"Better than I did." He took a breath. "It was a good job. Good firm. Great pay, even for a newbie like me. It was the work."

"I know about job stress."

"You do. But it wasn't the hours. I like the law." He returned to his silence. After a moment, he looked at her. "I really do. But I think I know what it was."

"What happened?" Taylor held up a hand. "Wait a sec. JJ, I'm your friend. I don't have my counselor's hat on. Sure, I'll encourage you to go in a healthy direction like I would with any good friend. Or even my family, if the dummies would listen. But if you have something to work out, maybe you need to be talking with your shrink."

"Haven't seen him in months," he said. "I'm not looking for a counselor. Just want to talk it a little and see how it sounds to me. You don't even have to say anything if you don't want to."

"All right. Go for it."

"It goes back to the '90s, back in Ohio. I met Karen on a task force chasing some drug makers. The methamphetamine wave was just coming into sight." He paused and sipped at his cola.

"Motorcycle gang, Steel Riders, they were very big in it. They got into a shoot-out and a little girl was accidentally killed. Stray round. They got off on a technicality. Shortly after the case was thrown out, Steel Riders starting getting killed." He frowned, remembering. "We thought it was a rival gang. Being just a county deputy sheriff, they had me doing footwork on the outside chance it might have been someone else." He took a breath and the silence returned.

Taylor said nothing, leaning back in her chair. From somewhere, probably the professor's apartment, music gently wafted. Classical, maybe Bach. It carried the smell of bacon. The professor was a traditionalist in several ways.

"The Riders felt we were pushing too close. They ambushed one of our cars. Killed a friend of mine, FBI guy, and wounded another friend, a fellow county deputy. Almost got Karen." Another pause. Taylor's eyes were wide.

13

"I figured I knew who was taking down the Riders, the ones where the little girl died. I didn't realize that for sure until the day I found the meth lab. They had it in a farm. While I watched, two people, two relatives of the little girl, showed up. I wasn't sure what to do and while I sat there with my brain up and locked, the two took the Riders out, including their leader, the last of the five involved in the girl's death. Just like that. Just a couple of Ohio good-old boys" (he pronounced it "Oh-hiah") "taking out the trash."

"What happened?" Taylor frowned. "Did you have to arrest them?"

"Not exactly," Jeffers said. He leaned his head back, taking the last few drops of soda as if they were medicine. He put the can down and paused before he looked at Taylor. "Not for attribution," he said.

"Not a problem," Taylor replied, nodding.

"I covered it up, tampered with evidence, kept my mouth shut. Anyway, I decided being in law enforcement was not a good idea for me. Not playing by cop rules. Better to work on the justice side." He fell silent, his eyes looking towards the horizon and Taylor waited.

"Karen knew, knows, whatever." He took a breath. "Supported me going to law school; she understood I had to get out of law enforcement." He shook his head. "After what she'd been through… Anyway, I got out of school and got a good job with a Philly firm."

"Good job," Jeffers said, repeating himself. "But…"

He paused and Taylor wondered at his reluctance to speak – he had just shared covering up what sounded like a crime.

"But the firm had a big chunk of criminal law practice in addition to everything else. That's where they put me." He smiled but his eyes did not show it. "That's where I put myself. Working on keeping bad guys, and they were almost all bad guys, out of jail. Maybe being an ex-cop wasn't the best thing to be for that. I made a lot of money for me and the firm and I drank more and more and Karen finally had enough."

Taylor said nothing, sensing something else was there.

"I got a man off," Jeffers said. "Technicality but a first-year law student would have spotted it. The prosecution should have, didn't. It was dismissed and I was at my table, stuffing my briefcase, the defendant gone, the judge gone, and I sat down and couldn't stop the tears." He shook his head. "That's how it had started in Ohio, some punk biker getting off on a technicality. Karen had been gone about three months by then. I went to my first meeting that night." He looked at the cooler. "One day at a time."

Taylor could not think of anything to say that would solve anything. She reached over and lightly punched JJ in the arm.

"Damn," she said softly. He nodded.

Taylor regarded Jeffers as a friend, a designation with which she was sparing. She didn't know how that happened – being white, male, and hetero, were its roots in his being "safe," whatever the hell that meant? Possibly that opened the door, but it was his *steadiness*, that's the word she had settled on months ago, and his willingness to listen when she needed to talk.

He *listened*, she decided, like he meant it. He didn't look for ways to get the conversation back to him, he didn't miss what she said at all of its levels, and he didn't try to steer her away from things that he might have found uncomfortable. Or hurry into giving her the solution.

When Taylor talked about her sometimes-rocky relationship with Marianne, as she just had, whatever else was going on, she knew he supported her. The gentle teasing they both used was a sign, she knew, of trust. JJ, as she usually thought of him, was her surrogate big brother. A tall, *white* big brother.

Another thing, she thought and smiled, that would appall her family.

"How did you get this place?" she asked. "You never said."

"Severance and savings, Roth and 401K," JJ said. He reached into the cooler and brought out a brown bottle. He grinned at it. "Amish birch beer," he said. "Evidence of the existence of a supreme being."

"I've had it," she said, shaking her head. "You gave one to me a couple of weeks back. It tastes like cat piss. A cat in poor health."

"What would a North Philly girl know about birch beer?" He twisted the lid off and took a swallow. "Outstanding."

"So, what's the deal?" Taylor asked. "You being a landlord, that's just so you can hide?"

"You might be right," JJ replied. "Not ready to go back into the deep end of the pool just yet."

"You just talking about being a lawyer?"

"No, don't think so." He looked at her and smiled. "You sure you're not being a shrink?"

For his part, Jeffers liked Taylor from the day he met her. He had just walked outside with his contractor when she drove up. She was, she said as she got out of her totally sensible Toyota Corolla, looking for an apartment. She wore a conservative suit and a Veterans Administration ID hung from a "Veterans Are Why America is No. 1" lanyard around her neck.

15

Mark, JJ's contractor, said she had come to the right place and said she would particularly like the paint. Grinning, he climbed into his big truck and exchanged waves with JJ as he drove away.

"He's just bragging," JJ said. "Let me show you what we have."

She liked the two-bedroom apartment on the second floor, particularly when she looked out the window and saw a river going past.

"Branch of the Brandywine River," JJ said. "You crossed it coming here. Harder to see from the ground floor because of the trees."

"Who else is here?" she asked.

"Upstairs, just me," he said. "Across from you is a history prof, University of Pennsylvania. Only have one apartment taken downstairs. Pair of psychology students…"

"From the VA medical center," she said, nodding. "I know them, they told me about the apartment."

"Free advertising," he said. He pulled a sheet of paper from his clipboard and handed it to her. "Details, utilities, cable, all that, what passes for rules around here, rates. Stone building, pretty old, sound usually isn't a problem. Parking you saw, we have a plow service. If you have a lot of friends coming over, it's ok to have them park in the grassy area across the road. Time to time, we have the grill going, everyone potlucks it." He smiled. "The prof does a killer Texas bar-be-que brisket."

"The painting was well done."

"I'll tell Mark you said that," he said. "Do you want it?"

"Yes," she said. "What do I call you?"

"Mostly it's 'JJ,'" he said. "'Mister Jeffers,' is fine, or, if you prefer, 'Hey, you!'"

She nodded, studying the sheet. Finally, she raised her eyes.

"Just one thing," she said. "I don't keep it a secret."

"You play in a rock band?" He frowned. "I'd keep that a secret, too."

"No," she said, grinning in spite of wanting to be serious. "I'm gay."

"Thank god," JJ said. "Those rockers, at landlord school they told me to watch out for them. Noisy."

"It's not a problem?"

"No, ma'am," JJ said, the levity gone from his voice. His eyes were steady and he did not look away. "It's not."

"I'll take the apartment."

"That's not a problem, either."

She smiled with the memory, remembering that JJ had not asked for her name until that point. Taylor, still smiling, started to say something – she would never remember what it was – when her cell phone buzzed. She took it out and everything changed.

Forever.

Chapter 4

Across the fishing lake from the trailer park, a woman in an expensive, large log cabin stared into a steel sink holding shattered pieces of a dropped dish.

"Fuck."

It was all she said for a moment. Her lips were tight, as if holding back everything else she might say. Her eyes remained on the small dish. It lay in pieces and if she had been poetic, she might have drawn an analogy to her life.

But she wasn't and didn't. Carefully, she picked up the shattered ceramic shards – they could be sharp as glass, she had learned from previous encounters with broken things – and then dropped them into the trash can under the sink.

She ran the water into the sink, making sure all the small fragments were washed away. Then she turned off the water and, her hands on the edge of the sink, stared out the window towards the lake.

Her reflection looked back and it looked like she felt – a white face, drawn tightly across cheekbones, brown eyes angry but steady, a mouth held small with tension, thin smile lines that were shallow, as if not used much, the whole face crowned with short, shaggy dark brown hair that suggested she did not care much about her appearance.

She looked at her self and saw the anger and tension. Slowly she stuck her tongue out.

"So, there," she said to her reflection, making a small smile before turning away.

The kitchen area opened onto the large dining room. Wood was everywhere, light on the walls, hard under foot, dark for the furniture. The living room, off of which three bedrooms lay, was dominated by a flat screen television that competed for attention with a stone fireplace that could have accommodated a compact car.

She flopped onto a leather couch and picked up her to-do list from an end table. Almost everything on it was crossed off. Still had to get some coffee and milk. The last item, getting the snow blower its post-winter check by the local dealer, remained pending its return from the shop. She put the paper down and picked up yesterday's mail.

Most were ads for one thing or another, all addressed to the owner, Mister Lowenstein. She always called him "Mister" though he had told her more than once that she could call him Mel now that she was no longer working in his furniture store.

Using the title was a distancing tactic – that's what her counselor had said and she was right. She wasn't worried about Lowenstein coming on to her, it was just that letting anyone close…

She flipped through the envelopes and then stopped when she came to one marked:

Ms. Elizabeth Chernov

It was from the Veterans Administration Medical Center in Coatesville. She looked at it for a moment and then opened it.

Inside was a form letter telling her she had missed her last outpatient appointment and attempts to contact her by telephone had failed and would she please contact the clinic to set up her next appointment?

Chernov nodded; she had not missed her appointment; she had chosen not to go. That was four weeks ago. They finally had noticed.

She folded the letter up into ever decreasing squares. It wasn't the counselor's fault. Nice lady, used that eye movement stuff. It was just that going in every other week for a half hour session felt like a waste of time and there were people who needed the time more than her. Besides, the nightmares were pretty much gone and she hadn't had a drink in five months and four days.

Maybe she could go into town, pick up the coffee and milk. Get out of this cabin that she was baby-sitting for Mr. Lowenstein and get some fresh air. That brought a small smile. Here she was, in the middle of nowhere, forest, lake, and she was thinking about needing fresh air.

Better than being down range…

She pulled her mind away from the unbidden thought and focused on getting her keys. They were in her bedroom, sitting in the small bowl on her chest of drawers.

She pulled down a black, hooded windbreaker with the arced word ARMY in gold on the back from its hanger. "It's just a jacket," her counselor had said and she finally had accepted the idea, more or less.

As she left her bedroom, she checked that all the house lights were off. They were hardly needed with the large windows but there was no sense running up the bill for Mr. Lowenstein. She paused as she pulled on the jacket and decided to check on the night light over the back deck – she had left it on all day a week ago and didn't want to make that mistake again.

Chernov stepped out onto the back deck as she worked on the zipper. Glancing up, she saw the light was out. She turned. With the trees and brush she could just see the lake. Naturally, there was no one out on it, especially not in the spring morning cold, but that would change as people filtered into the cabins encircling the water. Lots of vacationers, rod and reel people; as things warmed up they would appear. From where she stood, she couldn't see any neighbors. Lowenstein owned a good chunk of the lake front and his kids and their kids and their friends were a bit like a traveling circus when they finally appeared after school let out. She guessed they needed the space.

Chernov started to turn to go back into the house when she saw movement down at the lake's edge. She stopped, her eyes steady. The glimpse of green was not from nature. Jacket, probably. She waited.

The girl slowly appeared, the bushes obscuring her so that it was like she materialized. She moved in a crouch, looking around, and when she saw the path up to the cabin, she instinctively moved to it.

"Fuck," Chernov said for the second time that day.

"Fuck," Books said, unknowingly echoing Chernov. He looked around, working on catching his breath. As he did, his cellphone buzzed.

"Anything?" Jacks asked.

"Not yet," he said. "Where are you guys?"

"Coming up on the intersection of the road north of the lake," Jacks said. He was calm, calmer than Books felt after walking around the west side of the lake and through every damned thorn bush in Pennsylvania. "Have you seen anyone?"

"No," Books replied. He started walking again, earning him an angry look from Jonesy. Books cocked the phone so Jonesy could hear both sides of the conversation. "Hard to see most of the houses from the lake but the ones we could didn't look occupied." He paused and then added, "Big fucking lake."

"Keep going, Books," Jacks said, using his name. "You must be driving her forward. We're turning now. We'll go down one of these driveways and block her."

"Yeah," Books said. "Is he sure he saw the right girl?"

"No question," Jacks said. He seemed confident in the driver. "We have the product, just need the cash. Keep going."

"All right," Books replied. He looked at Jonesy as he put his phone away. "We keep going," he said.

"No kidding," Jonesy said, his expression still angry. "I heard him." Maybe he was jealous that Jacks called Books by name, a thought that brought a grin to Books' face that made Jonesy look even angrier.

Books decided to say nothing else. He figured the girl had taken off in some other direction, maybe even to one of the other trailers, or drowned her ass in the lake. Stumbling around in the forest did not seem to him to be a very bright move. Someone had to have heard the shooting and he thought it likely they had punched 911 into their phone. By now there would be police on the way.

Sure, they were out in the boondocks. Most of the small towns had no police and a few of those that did just had part-timers that did traffic duty. But Chester County had a Sheriff's Office and they did more than manage the courtrooms down in West Chester. And the state troopers could get anywhere pretty damned fast. With a report of gunfire, it would not be just one deputy or trooper.

There was nothing to be done for it except keep going. Books licked at the back of a thorn-scratched hand. It wasn't going to be fun, hadn't been, but nailing the kid would really add to his reputation.

That really mattered, he reminded himself. It didn't matter how good you thought you were or even how good you were, not really. Books understood the world worked on the basis of how good people thought you were. He nodded to himself as he stepped over some red-brown arms of a thorn bush. If someone like Jacks thought he was reliable, then he was really in. Even Tallman would take notice of him.

"House over there," Jonesy said, keeping his voice down and pointing through the trees. Books squinted, looking up hill.

"Yeah," he said. "Doesn't look like anyone's home." He glanced in the other direction. "Belongs to that dock." He thought for a moment. "They cut out all the brush, no cover. She wouldn't go in that direction, can't hide. I think she's still circling the lake."

"Whatever you say," the other man said and it hit Books that the other man was following his lead.

21

That meant he was dumping the responsibility on Books. For a second, Books felt his heart beat with fear but then it lessened a little. This was how you got into the big leagues.

"We keep going," Books said, his voice firm. Jonesy just shrugged but he obeyed and Books' fear melted like wax in a fire.

"Hey," Chernov said, slightly raising her voice. The little girl – she looked to be less than ten years old – did not respond. "Hey." That caught her attention and her head jerked up like a faun in the woods.

She sort of was, Chernov thought. The little girl looked terrified, exhausted and terrified, and unable to decide whether to run. The blue backpack she wore looked heavy and had probably added its two-cent contribution to her exhaustion.

"You're trespassing," Chernov said. She shook her head. "You're not allowed here. Go home."

The girl still said nothing, frozen half way between the house and the lake.

"Go on," Chernov said. She frowned. The girl was trembling, though with fatigue or fear or some combination she could not tell. "Who are you?"

The girl looked behind her, down towards the lake, and when she looked back the terror had burned through the exhaustion.

"Fuck me," Chernov said, barely whispering. She shook her head and walked to the steps. "What's going on?" she asked in a normal voice. The girl took a hesitant step towards her.

Chernov kept walking forward down to the path and the girl, her lips tight, looked at her for a moment as if deciding something very important. Then she gathered strength she did not appear to have from some place and ran towards Chernov.

Startled, Chernov stopped but the girl did not. She ran into Chernov and grabbed her around her waist. She kept saying one word over and over.

"Please."

Chernov looked around but saw nothing even as her unconscious hands found the girl's shoulders and held her lightly.

"Come on," Chernov finally said, resignation in her voice. "Come with me."

The girl, silent tears running down her face, a face smeared with dirt and the red lines from the berry bushes found around the lake, did not release her grip on Chernov's legs so much as permit Chernov to transfer her grip to one of the woman's hands. The girl held on tightly, someone holding onto a lifeline at sea, but walked with Chernov back up the slope and onto the deck.

Chernov paused, looking back towards the lake, but saw nothing. She led the girl into the house.

"House up there," Books said quietly and Jonesy paused to search for it.

"Yeah, got it," he said. He pointed to one side. "Path going up."

"You see any lights?"

"None. Looks deserted, like the others. You wanna go up there?"

Books thought for a moment and then shook his head.

"No. I figure she's still running." He pulled out his phone. "I'll let Jacks know where we are but let's keep going."

Chernov walked into the living room, the little girl still holding her hand. She didn't bother with the lights as she steered the child to a leather-covered chair whose size emphasized the girl's smallness.

"All right now," Chernov said as the girl, her eyes still wide, sat down. "What's your name?"

The girl remained silent for a moment but Chernov did not try to fill the silence. Finally she spoke, her voice low.

"I'm Sherrie," she said. "That's for Sharon."

"Glad to meet you," Chernov said. She held out her hand. "My name is Elizabeth." The two shook hands.

"My full name," she added, "is Elizabeth Chernov. What's yours?"

"Sherrie Stuart," the girl said almost automatically. She looked around. "Is this your house?"

"No," Chernov said, smiling slightly. "I'm just house-sitting. Do you live in one of the houses?"

"Trailer." Sherrie looked away.

Chernov paused. There was a trailer park that had been going out of business for a while now. It was almost directly across the lake. On the other hand, a few of the fisher folk had trailers on their small plots. It made no difference. She had enough to get the necessary wheels rolling. She stood up.

"You hungry, want something?" she asked. The little girl shook her head. "Do you know your number? I can call your parents."

"I was supposed to wait," Sherrie said, "but I heard guns so I ran away." Suddenly tears ran from her eyes but she said nothing else.

23

"Guns?" Chernov's own eyes widened slightly. "At your trailer?"

Sherrie just nodded.

"Sherrie, what happened?"

"I don't know," the little girl said, and it sounded like she was blaming herself for not knowing. "Mom told me to get in the hiding place like we practiced before and I waited just like I was supposed to," her voice turned into a plea, "but I heard the guns so I ran."

"All right," Chernov said, as her mind raced. She came to no conclusions except one. She walked over to a table and picked up a telephone. She punched in numbers she knew by heart.

"East Joyton Borough Police," a woman's voice said on the second ring.

"Hi, Ann. It's Elizabeth. Listen, is Don working?"

"Sure is, got the day watch supervision. Want me to punch you through?"

"Please, thanks."

Chernov heard a sequence of familiar clicks and then a man's deep voice.

"Sergeant Donald Brunner," he said. "How may I help you?"

"Don, Elizabeth."

"Hey, Beth, how the hell are you?

"Doing fine, doing fine."

"Captain Peterson was asking about you just last week," Brunner said. "He'd really like to get you back on board."

"Hey, thanks," Chernov said. "Maybe I'll come by and we can talk about it."

"That would be great," Brunner said. "We could use an experienced hand around here to straighten out all the things I've messed up. So, anyway, what's up?"

"Don, you got any missing child reports?"

"Missing child? I don't think so but let me double-check for alerts from the Sheriff's Office. I know there's nothing here in town. Just a second... No, nothing like that. There's a big thing east of you but no missing children. Want me to check the state?"

"No, this is local." Chernov took a breath. "I've got a young girl here, white, age ten or less, brown and brown, red sneakers, blue jeans, green t-shirt, gray windbreaker, blue backpack. She gives her name as Sharon Stuart."

"Got it."

"Here's the thing. She said she fled her home, a trailer, when she heard guns firing."

"Shit."

"Yeah. I don't know if it was a domestic thing or…"

"Hold a sec. Let me check county for any reports on gun fire. Tapping into the computer. Trailer… I remember there's an old trailer park across the lake from you."

"Could be it."

"Got it," Brunner said. "911 call about 25 minutes ago, yeah, the area is a match for that trailer park. Shots fired, no details. County deputies responded. Let me check… Yes, there is a Stuart listing for one of the trailers. Did she give any indication of what happened?"

"She said her mother told her to hide but did not say from what. When she heard the guns, she took off. She looks like she ran all the way around the lake."

"Damn. All right, I will notify the deputies. They'll pick her up. Are you going to be at the cabin?"

"Yes."

"All right." Brunner paused. "She all right?"

"No apparent physical injuries," Chernov said.

"Yeah. All right," he repeated. "I'll pass the word. If I get an ETA, I'll let you know."

"Thanks, Don."

"No problem, Beth."

Chernov put the telephone down and let out a long breath, realizing part of the tension she had felt in making the call came from questions that neither Ann nor Brunner had asked. Well, the issue of the girl, of Sharon, naturally occupied attention a little more than her sobriety or therapy.

"You sure you don't want anything to eat or drink?" she asked the girl. Sharon just shook her head. Chernov sat next to her.

"I called a friend of mine," she said. "He's a policeman." Sharon's eyes went wide with alarm. "It's all right," Chernov quickly added. "He's a good guy. I've known him around nine years. He works over at East Joyton."

Sharon nodded but it wasn't clear at what.

"He said the county deputies are checking out your home and they would probably want to talk to you."

Sharon remained silent, her eyes staring into Chernov's.

"If everything's okay," Chernov said, "they'll probably take you home." The statement sounded hollow to Chernov but the little girl did not look away. "It's going to be all right," she added, and that sounded hollow, too.

Whatever happened back at your trailer, little girl, the one place they are not going to take you for a while is home, Chernov thought. It bothered her that she wasn't being straight with the girl but she didn't know what else to say. She stood up abruptly.

"I was getting ready to go shopping," she said. "I'll check that the back door is locked and then after the sheriff deputies come to help you, I'll go take care of that."

Sharon remained silent but her eyes lowered until she was staring at the floor. Chernov hesitated and then turned away.

Angry but unable to say why, Chernov walked through the kitchen to the back door. The sliding door to the deck was closed and she flipped the latch, locking it. Movement down the path caught her eye and she saw two men.

One had a gun in his waistband.

Chapter 5

JJ drove Aretha to the identification and stood behind her as the curtains were drawn back. Her hands were at her mouth immediately and her sob, cut off, sounded like it strangled her. She weaved and JJ held her elbow, lightly, just with his fingertips. He wasn't an anchor; his touch was more like a distant lighthouse seen at night, offering a sense of direction, its flash not controlling but reassuring.

"It's her," she said, the words forced, and the plain clothes state trooper nodded. The curtain slid silently back and then Aretha turned into JJ's chest and she cried.

The two state police officers, one in the gray uniform, the other in a suit, waited with the patience that police officers develop. After a moment, Aretha looked up and JJ handed her a handkerchief.

Only the plain clothes officer asked questions. JJ heard his name as Philip Ross though Aretha missed it. A tall black man with hair turning white around his temples, he was brief.

Aretha told them when she had last seen Marianne, when she had last talked to her, the nature of their relationship – neither trooper showed a reaction when she said, "Lovers" – and that she did not know anyone who disliked her. She volunteered that they had had an argument the last time they talked. The troopers nodded but did not ask for details.

Ross then said Marianne's family had been notified but, since her mother could not travel and her brother would not arrive until early evening, they had needed her for the identification. Aretha nodded and JJ cocked his head slightly to one side.

"How did you know of her relationship," JJ asked, "with Ms. Taylor?"

"Ms. Taylor is listed," Ross said, "in her emergency notification paperwork at her agency."

JJ nodded and said nothing. Ross looked at him for a moment but then turned to Aretha.

"We are sorry for your loss," he said. He paused. "There's a chance that other officers, federal agents, may need to talk to you."

Aretha nodded and then they were gone.

JJ said nothing as they drove away from the hospital. He found himself wishing, for some reason, that it was summer. He needed warmth.

"JJ," Aretha said, her voice revealing little interest and her eyes staring out the passenger's window, "why were the state police there?"

"In Pennsylvania," JJ said, grateful for something to break the silence, "where isolated communities don't have police coverage, it's sometimes provided by the troopers." He paused, checking his rearview mirror. "A lot of the smaller towns and boroughs, it's been a hard decade and they've cut back services and got rid of their police or share costs with other boroughs."

"I thought the state troopers just chased speeders."

"They do that," JJ said, "but their Bureau of Criminal Investigation is pretty sharp. Good lab services, forensics, all of that kind of thing as well."

"Do you think they'll find who did it?"

JJ remained silent for a moment, trying to decide what to say, and then mentally shrugged.

"They have someone in mind already," he said. As she turned and looked at him, he quickly added, "I mean, I think they have someone in mind."

"How do you know that?"

"Damned few questions for you," he said. "That suggests they are not fishing for leads since they have a good one."

"So they know who did it?"

"More like they know of who did it."

"I don't understand."

"They might have a particular person in mind," JJ said. "They may be out beating the bushes for him right now. On the other hand, they might not have a specific identification, not yet, but they know enough about the crime to know you are neither a suspect nor someone who is likely to know who did it. That's why they were so quick with you, though they may talk more later."

"'Know enough...'" She shook her head. "I think I know too much." Aretha turned away and pressed her head against the glass. Then she turned back.

"What would they know that would make them not need to ask me a lot of questions?"

"Well," JJ said, and then stopped. "Look, this may not be something to talk about, not now. Maybe later."

"Tell me."

"All right," JJ said after another pause. "One reason they don't need to ask you a lot of questions is this is not the first murder the killer has done. So they already know of him." He glanced at her; her face was carved of stone. "Federal agents also suggest they think this has happened in more than one state."

"I see."

JJ glanced at Aretha. She sat with her eyes closed, her hand pressed against her mouth, not a stone unless stones dropped tears, and he clenched his teeth in anger at his stupidity.

Chapter 6

As Jeffers and Aretha stood near a dead body, Books listened intensely to Jacks, pressing his cellphone tightly against his ear. Jonesy was still walking ahead but stopped when he heard Books' impatient snapping of his fingers.

"Got it," Books said, lowering his hand. "We'll check it out." He flipped the phone shut and stuffed it back into his pocket. Jones raised his eyebrows in an unspoken question.

"Mister Jacks says the kid's in one of these houses," Books said. Jonesy looked alarmed and pulled his pistol from underneath his jacket.

"How the fuck does he know that?"

"Doesn't matter," Books said. "And put that damned thing away." Jonesy complied, jamming the pistol back into its holster, his expression sullen.

"He's going to the house, got the number somehow, and we're supposed to get up to the road. Watch for the SUV and cover things."

Jonesy nodded and turned and looked up the path.

"Looks like this will take us up there."

Books looked up towards the house, one of those rich people's places made out of logs. He didn't see any lights on but for a second he thought he saw a gray shadow behind the sliding door opening to the deck. He blinked and it was gone.

"Yeah," Books said. "Let's go."

Chernov reflexively turned away from the door and strode back to Sharon. Though anxiety surged in her, her voice was calm, almost flat, as she held out her hand to the girl.

"Tell you what," she said as she almost pulled Sharon to her feet. "Let's not wait here. Let's go for a ride."

Chernov knew she wasn't making much sense but her voice seemed to command obedience and Sharon stepped quickly along with her as they walked through the living room and out the front door.

A few more steps had them at Chernov's old Honda hatchback. She lifted Sharon into the passenger seat and buckled her in, wishing the girl had taken her backpack off but unwilling to take the time now.

She deliberately but quickly, with no wasted motion, slid in behind the wheel and started the car. She did not bother with her own seat belt and backed the Honda onto a curving path, pointing it towards the road almost a hundred yards away.

Chernov took the turn onto the road almost too fast but she handled the slide easily as the car turned east. The road had country road dips and rises with the occasional curve suggesting the whole thing was little more than pavement poured over some half-forgotten Indian trail.

As they came around a curve, Chernov saw a big SUV coming west and less than two hundred yards ahead.

"Sharon," she said, "get down."

"What?"

Chernov did not repeat herself. Instead, she reached the little girl's far shoulder and pulled her flat and held her down awkwardly, her backpack twisting her.

As the two cars passed, Chernov glanced at it. The heavily tinted windshield revealed little but she saw through the driver's side window, dimly, a bearded man driving. He was staring at her while, beyond him, hovering ghost-like, she thought she saw another man, white, thin, and then they were gone.

Her eyes were on the rearview mirror but there was no flare of brake lights from the SUV – it continued on its way as if in calm counterpoint to her own sense of fear.

"Please." Sharon's terrified voice intruded and Chernov lifted her hand. How hard had she been pressing down?

"Sorry," she said.

Almost immediately, like an orchestra edgily waiting for its cue, Chernov, her lips tight, began berating herself.

Why had she run away? Two men walking around the lake meant, what? Nothing, nothing that could be proved. *But there was a gun.* Immediately, she questioned what she saw. In any case, her reflexes kicked in and it was like she could not control herself. The idea of losing control was The Issue, as her counselor had said. So what was going on? Did any of this have anything to do with what Sharon said? Was she telling the truth?

Her lips were still tight even as she admitted to herself she did not know, but her reaction left her angry at no one and everything, including herself.

Especially including herself.

"Are you mad at me?" the girl asked in a voice that made her seem even smaller.

"What?" Chernov was surprised and she looked for a second at Sharon. "God, no. I'm not mad at you." As she spoke, she felt the anger and tension drain, flowing back into its hiding place somewhere behind her heart.

"I didn't know who was in the car," Chernov said slowly. "I guess I thought they might be bad people." Her lips tightened slightly. "Probably just a couple of guys looking for a place to rent for fishing."

"You were mad at them?"

"No, not really." Chernov felt a flash of irritation and took a deep breath and held it as she steered the Honda around a pothole.

"You see," she said slowly, "I get worried about things, like people I don't know. I'm not supposed to, but I do." She glanced at Sharon. "See?"

"Why?"

How the fuck am I supposed to know? The words remained unspoken as mental brakes slammed on.

"Well," Chernov said, "part of it is from being a police officer." She looked at Sharon, whose eyes widened slightly in surprise. "I'm not one anymore," she quickly added. "The biggest part was being in the Army. I was in the war."

"You were in Iraq?"

"Yes, twice," Chernov said. "You know about Iraq?"

"The teacher talked about it in class."

"No shit."

"No shit," Sharon said. She paused. "I'm not supposed to say that word. We have a couple of kids in school who have parents in the Army. Margaret's dad is a Ranger; she says they're the best."

"They're pretty good," Chernov said, glancing in the rearview mirror. She saw nothing.

"What were you in?"

"MPs," Chernov said. "I just directed traffic and gave people speeding tickets."

"Really?"

"Pretty much," Chernov said.

Chernov was silent for a moment. Ahead she saw the intersection for the road that bordered the lake's east side. Turning right would be the way to go to get to the trailer park, where she figured just about every cop in the county would be. She let the car roll to a stop.

On the other hand, the alarm that had led her to get out of the house was still muttering. Something wasn't right. It was stupid and didn't make any sense but she was very reluctant to go against it.

But heading to the police was the smart move. She pulled out her cellphone and tapped in the East Joyton police number. In a moment, she was talking with Brunner.

"Hey, Don, it's me."

"Okay, what's up?

"Where's the cavalry?"

"The who..? Oh, I get it." Brunner snorted in a semi-laugh. "Sorry for the delay but the Sheriff hasn't kicked anyone loose yet. There's only one trooper there and everyone's still securing the scene."

"I'm not at the house."

"You're not at the house," Brunner repeated back, as if not certain what he had heard. "Where are you?"

"In my car," Chernov said. "I saw two men at the lake. One was armed, so we left."

"Armed? Descriptions?" Brunner's voice was quick.

"Both white, looked to be average height and weight. The one with the gun had a thin beard. Both in jeans. The one with the gun, pistol, wore a black windbreaker. Long hair, shaggy, maybe black, covered his ears. The other blue jacket. Brown hair. They were coming towards the house."

"Got it. Look, I'm going to get the Sheriff on the line right now. If she can't get someone free, screw it, I'll come myself."

"All…"

Chernov's reply was cut off as she looked at the mirror and saw the black SUV coming back.

"Shit," she hissed and floored the accelerator, dropping the cellphone onto the console. It bounced and disappeared as the Honda surged forward.

Books heard the Honda start and tried to run up the slope. Jonesy followed, though not as quickly. Books came around the corner of the house just in time to see red tail lights reach the road and turn right. Still jogging down the drive, he pulled out his phone and hit the speed dial.

"They may be headed at you," he said when Jacks answered. "We came up to a house, heading for the road, and saw a red car, hatchback, I think, drive away."

"What's the house number?"

"Don't know," Books admitted, looking over his shoulder. The front of the big house had no markings he could see. "Be at the mailbox in a second, get it from there." Talking while jogging was taking away his breath.

"Which way did they turn when they got to the road?"

"To the right," Books said. "That would be east, towards you."

"All right." Jacks seemed very calm. "Let's assume she's got the girl and heard enough that she's panicky. We'll… Damn." For a moment, there was silence and Books, pressing the cellphone to his ear so hard it hurt, wondered if they had lost the connection.

"We just went passed her," Jacks said. "No time to do anything. Saw a woman driver but not the kid. Maybe they are not who we are looking for. Got the number?"

Books slid to a halt; Jonesy was well behind him, struggling to catch up. For a second, Books could not find the number until he saw it was on a reflective panel screwed to the mailbox post.

"Two one nine six," he said.

"Damn," Jacks repeated himself. Again, there was silence. "All right, we're going to pick you two up."

"Then we go after her?"

"Probably not," Jacks said. "I see you," he added. "Talk more in the car."

The connection ended and Books put away his cellphone. He looked over at Jonesy, who had given up trying to run and was walking.

"He's picking us up," Books said and motioned with his head. "That's him."

Jonesy nodded in acknowledgment and made no attempt at speaking.

"I think things are really fucked up." Jonesy nodded again as the SUV pulled over next to them. They got in as quickly as they could.

"I talked with Mister Tallman," Jacks said as the driver turned the SUV around, using the driveway. "He's not happy with all of it." Books felt his heart thud. "He's glad we got the product and put down those two but sees a big problem if the little girl saw anyone."

"He doesn't care we didn't get the money?" Jonesy asked and Books frowned. Now was not the time to be asking questions.

"He can live without it," Jacks said, apparently undisturbed by the interruption. "The problem is having all of us drop out of sight until we know what the girl saw."

"'Drop out of sight'?" Books couldn't help himself. Jacks smiled.

"Just that. Don't sweat it. Slip on down to Florida and enjoy the sand. We have a good shot at finding out what she knows pretty quickly. The only one of us who ever saw her might be the only person she could have seen." The driver stared at Jacks for a second before getting his eyes on the road again. "But I think she took off when she heard the guns and never looked back. As I said, don't sweat it. If things go all right, we'll know what she knows. We…"

"Holy shit," the driver said. "That's them."

"Go!" Jacks said, almost a yell.

The driver slammed the accelerator to the floor and the big Chevrolet immediately picked up speed. Books looked ahead and saw the red Honda turning left in a hard turn while its front wheels spun, bit into the pavement, and then leapt ahead.

The SUV's speed worked against it and the driver had to slow down to negotiate the turn.

"We have to force them off the road," Jacks said and Books saw his gun was out. He drew his own.

"Got it," the driver said.

They were gaining on the Honda – Books thought the smaller car should have been able to go faster – when it suddenly turned left and crossed the road. In a flash it was gone among the trees.

The SUV skidded to a halt.

"Fire road," the driver said. He backed up a few feet and then turned. The Honda was gone from sight, partially hidden by a turn in the fire road and by the dust it raised. He didn't hesitate and plunged ahead.

"Stay on her," Jacks said. His window slid down, letting in dust but he ignored it. Books saw the gun in his hand as he leaned his head out the window.

Books only caught glimpses of the Honda, a dark shape in the sprayed dirt and dust. It disappeared completely for a second and then red glowed like warning lights in a fog.

"Shit!" the driver yelled and the SUV skidded as the brakes slammed on. The dust was instantly gone, as if they had driven through a blanket and Books glimpsed tall trees in front of them.

For a heartbeat, Books thought they had made it, had missed the trees, when the SUV slapped him by jerking sideways. He hit the driver's seat and bounced back onto his own. There was a sound like a baseball bat hitting a trash can with his head inside and he bit his tongue as he bounced again.

Then everything was still, silent. Slowly, the dust caught up to them and thinly covered the SUV, dimming details. Silence, broken only by the turn indicator that had somehow come on, lay on them as the dust settled.

"Shit," the driver said, but this time it was said slowly, almost like a prayer.

"Let's go," Jacks said, looking out his window. "She turned right."

The driver started to back the SUV – Books was a little surprised it was still running – but stopped.

"Problem," he said as he pushed his door open. Books got out close behind him.

The left front fender was stove in, an obvious casualty to one of the trees. The metal pressed against the tire.

"Give me a hand," the driver said to Books and the two men reached down to pull the fender clear. It was hard to do as it cut into their hands and both men stopped to put handkerchiefs into their hands. "Ready, pull," the driver said, and slowly the bent metal pulled free of the tire.

The driver inspected their work and nodded. Both men got back into the SUV.

"We're good to go," the driver said.

"Don't think we're going to catch her," Jacks said, surprising Books with his apparent calm.

"Sorry, Mister Jacks," the driver said.

"May not be a problem," Jacks said. "I have to make a couple of calls. Go ahead and follow her. Maybe that damned bitch put herself into a tree. But first real road you come across, get us out of here."

"Back to Coatesville?"

"Yes," Jacks said. He shook his head. "She drove that thing like a Formula One racer." Oddly, he was smiling.

Books had heard of Formula One – some kind of European racing thing, he remembered – but he wondered what the hell Jacks found to smile about.

Chernov had seen the blur of the SUV in her side mirror as it failed to make the turn but she did not assume they were out of the chase. She drove as fast as she dared, more than once leaving the dirt track and scaring herself with the sudden, short fall back to the ground. But the Honda held up and she found old reflexes and skills kicking in.

She saw the paved road ahead and swung onto it already going faster than the posted speed limit. It took a second to orient herself and then she decided she was heading east. As good a direction as any.

Her eyes were on the rearview mirror but the SUV did not appear. She turned left onto a cross road – she missed the number – and now was heading north.

Ahead was a small village, several buildings hugging an intersection. This time she saw the sign – US 322 – and she turned onto it. If she stayed on it, it would take her all the way to Downingtown but it would cross US 30 just before, and 30 would take her to…

Her eyes darted down to the speedometer. Eighty-five miles per hour. No idea where she was going but she was getting there very quickly. She glanced in the rearview one more time and lifted her foot from the gas pedal.

So where was she going? Chernov glanced at Sharon. The girl's eyes were wide, though she looked otherwise more excited than scared.

"Sharon," she said, working to keep the adrenaline out of her voice, "can you see my cellphone?"

Sharon looked around and, after reaching down into the foot well, emerged holding the silver phone. Chernov took it, nodding in thanks, and saw a restaurant ahead. She slowed down and turned into its parking lot. She picked a parking space in the rear beside a large truck, partially blocking the view of them by anyone on the road.

Her connection to Brunner was gone. She punched the number in again and in a few seconds, she heard his voice.

"What happened?" Brunner asked.

"They showed up," Chernov said. "Dark blue Chevy SUV, tinted windows, didn't get the plates. They chased us until I lost them in the woods."

"Chased you?" There was a pause that Chernov made no effort to fill. "Are you sure?"

"I'm sure," Chernov said. "Followed us at high speed on the road and then a couple of forest roads. What's going on?"

"I don't know," Brunner said. "Look, I don't know what's happening but let's not take any chances. Let me come and get you. Where are you?"

Chernov opened her door and held up a hand to Sharon who nodded her understanding. She walked across the parking lot. Something was wrong, the alarm bell was going off and it had nothing to do with left over adrenaline from the chase. She paused at the corner of the restaurant and idly looked across the highway at a white-painted single story farm hardware store. A dozen cars and pickups sat in its parking lot.

"Are you there?" Brunner asked.

"Yeah," she said. "Just settling down the kid. I'm at the Brown Cow Restaurant, parked in front, right of the entrance."

"All right, stay in your car. I will come to you. I'll escort you to wherever the Sheriff wants to meet you. In the meantime, sit still and relax. I'm only fifteen minutes away."

"Don't you want to have the Sheriff send a deputy to me?"

"I don't want you on the road," Brunner said. Chernov heard tension in his voice. "If they see you, you might not outrun them again. And with the kid, it's probably better to wait."

"Got it," Chernov said. Brunner was making some sense.

"See you in a bit," Brunner said and the connection broke.

Chernov walked back to the Honda and sat down beside Sharon.

"That was pretty exciting," she said and the girl nodded.

"They were chasing me," Sharon said.

"Why would they do that?" Chernov said as she started the Honda. She looked around and slowly backed out of the slot.

"I have their money," Sharon said calmly, "and I have their pictures."

Chapter 7

Bob Guilder adjusted his glasses and looked again at the big display that showed the train arrival times. The high speed train from DC was on time; no surprise there. The Northeast Corridor trains generally met their schedules. The fact that a lot of politicians used them didn't hurt – even the Veep had commuted between DC and Maryland by train and Guilder guessed AMTRAK wasn't hurting for cash even if the rest of the government seemed to be sliding into the fiscal sea.

He smiled to himself, thinking he was getting cynical. Well, eleven years in the FBI could do that or worse to you. Or so people said. He doubted it was true. He liked his job, even when it meant, as it did now, standing around doing nothing but admiring the architecture of what everyone in Philadelphia called 30th Street Station.

You could have put a couple of full-sized houses in its big, open area. Stairs down to the tracks pierced the floor while a ramp off to one side led to the commuter train gates. His favorite place, the food court, occupied one side. He sipped at his berry and banana smoothie – he had friends who claimed a place near Drexel University made the best smoothies but he disagreed. The guys at 30th Street had the concoction nailed.

The big sign whirred, updating its arrivals. The train he waited for was five minutes out, matching nicely with the call he had received moments before. Special Agent Karen Deevers had talked to him twice on her trip up, the last time with a projection of her arrival time. So far she was on the money. Guilder sucked up the last of the smoothie and regretfully dropped his cup into a trash bin.

He walked to the head of the stairs. An AMTRAK employee waited, the stairs roped off and people already forming a line to board the train. Guilder pulled his identification out and, holding it low and using his body to block it from the line of people, showed it to the employee who showed little reaction other than a small nod before unhooking the velvet rope. Guilder quickly went down the steps.

The train came to the platform from around a distant, dark curve, and did so almost tentatively, as if bashful or perhaps a little embarrassed at being seen moving so slowly. Nonetheless, as it came alongside the platform and grudgingly came to a stop, its size and steadiness conveyed its strength. He glanced at his watch; exactly when Deevers projected her arrival.

Deevers had told Guilder which car she was on. As the door slid back, she stood before him, revealed by sliding aluminum like a magician's trick.

"Hey, Bob," she said as she stepped onto the platform, firmly steering a roller bag behind her.

"Good to have you back," Guilder replied. Deevers fell in beside him and he walked her to the stairs while other, more impatient, travelers streamed around them. They said little else; talking about cases while surrounded by civilians was unprofessional and their earlier conversations by cell phone had taken care of both agents' storage of polite conversation.

Guilder reached for her bag tentatively but Deevers shoved the extended handle down and picked up the bag without breaking stride. Guilder was not surprised; most women in the FBI made a point of not allowing men to treat them like civilian women. He still made the gesture, a left-over vestige of his conservative upbringing. He glanced at Deevers as they climbed the stairs but she showed no signs of being perturbed at his gesture and felt a small sense of relief. You never knew what might cause offense – then he paused and grinned. At least, *he* didn't always know.

A few minutes later they were in their car and making the entrance onto the Schuylkill Expressway, aka I-76. Guilder considered what he had seen of Deevers since he had joined the task force she was on. White, average height for a female, looked younger than her age, light brown hair tending to blond with a couple of silver hairs, cut short but without a great attention to style, slim build with muscles – she had carried her bag up the stairs from the platform effortlessly and he had adjusted it in the car's trunk, discovering it was heavier than she made it appear. Nice face, lines around her thin-lipped mouth suggesting she smiled a lot, though not since arriving in Philadelphia.

What else did he know? Currently she was assigned to Behavioral Analysis Unit Two, the group that studied crimes against adults by spree and serial killers and other offenses linked to multiple occurrences.

She was with the task force that was tracking a serial murderer – it had moved into Pennsylvania following a killing six weeks before and the one this morning had confirmed everyone's fear that their man was, in fact, in Pennsylvania.

Deevers was pretty intelligent, Guilder thought, and he assumed she was being groomed for bigger and better things. She had done a stint with the Hostage Rescue Team's Crisis Negotiation Unit and had been an instructor at Quantico, both prestigious positions. And earlier…

Almost two decades ago she had been in a county deputy sheriff's car with another FBI agent when they were ambushed by a drug gang. The deputy was badly wounded and the agent was killed but Deevers killed three of the perpetrators – it was said the only rounds she fired that didn't hit one of them were the ones she fired into their vehicle as they ran away.

Her work on the Behavioral Science Unit, her most recent assignment, was judged to be of the highest quality. Just last year she had been a profiler on the task force that hunted a serial killer who turned out to be a cop – he shook his head remembering all that had taken place here in southern Pennsylvania as well. Bringing her back for this task force had been a no-brainer.

The unofficial word seemed to confirm Guilder's impression that she was being prepared for advancement into the Bureau's upper management. Well, she seemed smart enough, judging by what she had been doing on the task force, and could shoot as straight as the occasion demanded, so she had Guilder's vote.

"Did you have a good time in DC?" Guilder asked. He grinned, showing he did not expect her to say yes and implying a compliment. The best agents in the field hated having to go to Washington, a place largely regarded, rightly or wrongly, as desired only by agents on the political make.

"Worked my butt off," she said. "But I think I got the information we wanted."

Guilder nodded; Deevers was a hard worker, that was certain. Also certain was her seriousness. He wondered if she had a life outside the job.

"It's nice to be back," she said.

"You've been here before. Before the task force, I mean."

"Yes," Deevers said. "I was in the Philly office a couple of years ago working with the regional HRT." She paused, as if considering something but added nothing else.

"The Staties have confirmed this latest one is by our guy."

"The marks?"

"Post-mortem, inner thighs. Same twist in the wires holding her to fence."

"Our forensic people on it?"

"And treading gently. The troopers don't miss much and we don't want them thinking we're second-guessing them."

"True. They picked up on the pattern, matching the first P-A crime with one down in Carolina and the other in Maryland. That's what got the task force up here."

"It was," he said.

Deevers nodded. "Some of the state agencies really have their acts together. That highway serial killing project started because of the Oklahoma Bureau of Investigation – they saw the patterns of women dumped along I-40 across multiple states."

"What's the count now?"

"VICAP says over 500."

"Damn."

"Roger that." She paused. "What's your take on how are the locals taking the bureau coming on board?"

"Generally, with good grace. The Chester County Sheriff is nobody's fool and was happy to have the Staties pile on and the troopers, when they picked up on the other two out of state, burned up the lines talking to us then and since it's been a hundred percent cooperation. No sign so far of anyone looking to make this a turf war. So nothing's changed since you went to DC. If anything, with this second killing they are even more happy to have us."

Deevers nodded. While publicity – the life blood of budgets – was one thing, in the face of serious cases, like a serial killer, most agencies worked more or less smoothly together. The FBI had made an art form on coordinating with state and local law enforcement. At least, it thought it had. There were still glitches and Deevers was aware most came about when the FBI stepped on toes unnecessarily.

Once the feds arrived, they were in charge and no one doubted that – but that didn't mean it was wise to shove people around; that encouraged leaks and would have an impact on future cooperation. Cops, whatever the uniform, worked hard at their jobs and were proud people.

Keep them in the loop, keep them working, and listen to them was the mantra now taught at the FBI Academy. She had a small piece of helping to change the FBI's attitude toward other law enforcement agencies and that only in part came from the fact she was married, separated but still married, to a former Ohio county deputy sheriff.

Deevers looked out the window, not really seeing anything. Six weeks ago, in the aftermath of the first Pennsylvania killing, she volunteered to come up with the task force. Did she do that so she would have a chance to see JJ? How did that make any sense at all, given that she had been dodging his calls for the past month? He had no idea she had been close by him all these weeks.

What had gone wrong? After Ohio, everything had seemed perfect. JJ in law school and pulling down a job with one of the more successful law firms in Philadelphia; that had gone so easily as to be almost miraculous.

Then the drinking… JJ was never abusive. Rather, he seemed to drift away, steadily getting further out of reach. The boat he was in seemed to follow a current that he didn't fight and she had never understood what was wrong.

Finally, she had given her ultimatum but nothing changed. Her bluff called, she left. She heard he quit the firm and she could only guess at what had happened – he never said.

Was leaving the right thing to do? The few people she knew still in touch with JJ said he had cleaned himself up, went to AA, and was now some kind of landlord. What did that mean and did she want to know?

"We're making good time," Guilder said, interrupting her thoughts. "The sheriff is giving us some more space in their new court building in West Chester, so we're out of those offices in Kennett Square. The sheriff posted an unmarked vehicle where it can watch the site in case our perp returns."

"He won't," Deevers said. "Glad to hear they followed our request, though."

"Don't they often return to where they dumped their bodies, trying to catch some of the thrill?"

"Some do, but he's not that kind."

"Oh? What kind is he?"

"Worse."

The word seemed to fill the car as Guilder drove on, silent.

Chapter 8

"Their money? Their pictures?" Chernov gripped the steering wheel hard enough that she thought the plastic-covered metal would bend but managed to get safely across the highway.

"In my backpack," Sharon said. "Mommy always kept the money in my old backpack. It was her friend Davy's but he got me a new one for school." She shrugged. "We always practiced. Get the pack, open the floor, hide under the trailer until Mommy or Davy said it was safe to come out." She looked down. "This wasn't practice."

Chernov said nothing as she drove slowly around the hardware store's parking lot. She found the driveway that took them around to the back of the building. A pair of empty loading docks, their doors down, and a closed steel door were the only features of the back wall.

She maneuvered the Honda so she could just see the front of the Brown Cow.

"Sharon," Chernov said, her eyes on the restaurant, "you've got their money in your backpack?"

"It's not really theirs," Sharon said. "It belongs to Mommy and Davy."

"May I see it?"

"Sure," Sharon said and started shrugging out of the backpack's straps. She had to stop and take off her seatbelt but finally handed it to Chernov. "Be careful," she said. "I put my phone in the side pocket. I took pictures." She patted her jeans. "I kept my iPod."

Chernov nodded and unzipped the blue backpack. She glanced down and then looked again. It was filled with money, rolls of bills held together with taut rubber bands. She put her hand in. The whole bag was crammed with money and...

Chernov felt the solid metal of a handgun, oddly warm to her touch. She pulled it slowly from the backpack.

"That's the other reason I wanted you to be careful," Sharon said. "I'm not allowed to touch it." She paused. "You shouldn't ever touch a gun if you don't know how to use it."

"I know," Chernov said. She looked at the restaurant – nothing had changed.

It rested in her hand as if its weight and solidness was a function of its awareness that it was held.

"Springfield Armory," she said, reading the insignia on the grip. "Model 1911-A1, .45 caliber." Her thumb punched the clip release and it smoothly slid out. Silver cartridge cases held brass bullets, each with a small, hollow gray cave in front.

She pushed the safety down and pulled the slide to the rear. A round ejected. It bounced into the backpack but she found it immediately, as if it did not wish to hide.

"One in the chamber? In a kid's backpack?" Chernov turned to Sharon. She studied the round. "Federal Hydra-Shoks. Is your Daddy an idiot?"

"Davy is not my Daddy," she said. She paused. "I don't have one. Not really." She took a breath. "Mommy and Daddy split up. Mommy said it wasn't about me." Her voice was low, almost a whisper, almost silenced by a child's guilt. "Mommy told me he went to New York and died."

Sharon hung her head and Chernov wondered if she was ever going to raise it; she could not find any words for the girl. Then she raised her head and looked at Chernov. There was something in her eyes, something that showed strength.

"But Davy is a friend of Mommy and he's okay." Sharon shrugged. "I explained. I only have that backpack when I go through the floor and hide. I have another for school."

"All right," Chernov said. She shook her head. She slid the clip back into the pistol. She flipped open the lid for the center console and put the pistol and spare round in, pushing down on the lid until she heard the slight click of the latch.

"We'll leave it there," she said and Sharon nodded.

"You said something about…" Chernov's voice trailed off as a dark blue Chevrolet SUV, its left fender showing a dent, eased into the Brown Cow's parking lot.

Her cell phone was in her hand as if by a magician's trick. Her thumb moved quickly through the menus to her contact list and found Brunner's cell number.

"Don," she said, her voice flat, "they're here."

"Don't panic," he said. "I'm two miles away, hitting the lights and siren. They'll probably jackrabbit when they see me. Don't try to run for it, I'll be right there."

"All right," Chernov said, her eyes on the SUV. She kept the connection open.

It did not stop but slowly circled the restaurant, as if a living thing. It reminded her of a scene from a movie she had seen. A movie with sharks.

The SUV stopped to one side of the restaurant. A passenger door opened and a young-looking man got out. It was a second before she recognized him as one of the two at the lake. He did not pause and walked into the restaurant. After a moment, he came out. He shook his head negatively before he climbed back into the car.

"Putting you on hold," Brunner said. "I'm a minute away and I'm letting the Sheriff know what's going on."

"Right," Chernov said. Her chest felt empty as if her heart had left. She cut the connection. She took a deep breath and let it out slowly. There had been nothing to hear, only the sound of passing traffic and the cold, indifferent wind.

No siren.

"Is something wrong?" Sharon asked and Chernov made a small laugh.

"Only the usual," she said.

"What the fuck?" Jacks finally showed impatience as Books closed his door.

"No little girl," Books said, "no single women. Everyone in there looked to be about eighty."

Jacks pulled up his cell phone.

"Hey, we're there," he said. "They're not." He was silent for a moment and then nodded. "What she said was untrue," he said calmly. "She lied to you. Which means two things. First, she doesn't trust you anymore. Second, and this is the part that I find very interesting, she picked up on you. Now, we already know she drives like she really knows how. What about this woman should I know?"

Jacks sat silently for a moment, interrupting only one time.

"For how long?

Books heard a tinny voice coming from Jacks' cell phone but could not make out what was being said. Finally, the voice stopped.

"Fucked up how?" Jacks asked.

The tinny voice began again but this time Jacks cut him off.

"All right," he said. "You need to be on your toes. Get your story very, very straight. If she gets to someone and starts talking, people are going to have questions for you." He paused letting the words sink in. "If she ever calls back, you call me directly, immediately. Clear?"

The tinny voice barely squeaked before Jacks closed his phone.

"Some days," he said, shaking his head. "Some days…"

Chernov watched the dark blue SUV. For several minutes, it sat as if uncertain as to what to do.

Welcome to my world, she thought.

"What are we going to do?" Sharon asked. "Is something else wrong?"

"The people who chased us are here," Chernov said, nodding towards the restaurant. "I don't want to move. They might see us."

"We're hiding," Sharon said, nodding.

"Right." Chernov grimaced. "And the person I counted on to help us, well, I don't know if he's on our side or theirs."

"He's your friend?"

"Once upon a time." Chernov squinted; the SUV was moving, pulling out onto the highway. She watched as it rolled east. "I was away with the Guard, couple of times. He kept me in touch with things, tried to make me feel welcome when I came home."

"Who was the guard?"

"No one," Chernov said, making a small, rare grin. "I meant National Guard, the Army." She paused. "I guess I was sort of a guard. I was military police."

"The Army have police?"

"Oh, yeah, they do" she said, still looking down the highway. "Since I was in the police here, being in the police in the Guard was kind of a natural fit." She eased the Honda from its hiding place; the SUV had disappeared into the distance.

"Davy says you can't trust the police."

"You can trust me," Chernov said, her voice emphatic and slightly surprising her. Then she grimaced. "And, yeah, Davy might be right about some police."

"What are we going to do?"

"What we need to do," Chernov said, pulling out onto 322 and turning away from the SUV, "is find someone you and I can trust to help us get to people who will take care of us."

"A friend of yours?"

"There's someone I know from a while ago."

"Another policeman?"

"No," Chernov said, making the small grin again, "someone even more untrustworthy. She's a journalist."

Chapter 9

"So there it is," Special Agent Karen Deevers said. "My little expedition to DC has added to our knowledge of the perpetrator." Behind her a PowerPoint projection glowed in silent corroboration of her words; the other agents and Pennsylvania law officers sat in the dimly lit room, their eyes locked on the display.

The red dots, each one neatly dated, appeared like a casually thrown string of fake pearls up the eastern United States. One in South Carolina, the first one. Eight in North Carolina. One in Tennessee. Then two more in Virginia. One in Maryland, dated less than a year ago.

And two in Chester County, Pennsylvania, one dated two months before and the other yesterday.

"It's the lack of similarities in method that kept it from being noticed?" an agent in back asked.

"Yes," Deevers said. "He has put other victims on display but the manner of the display has varied. The method of killing has varied as well. There are marks on the thighs, but not always. We think those are the ones he failed to penetrate sexually." She glanced to one side and made a barely noticeable nod towards the senior Pennsylvania State Police detective sitting at a table, his hands folded. "PA," she pronounced it "P – A," "caught the similarities with Maryland and one of the older ones in North Carolina. We had the other incidents, but they had not been made part of the string."

"The latest DNA has matched several," she said. "He's not particularly neat. Arrogant. But not stupid. He's tried to mix up his kills, different methods, but he has repeated himself a few times."

"The wire…" the agent said, nodding.

"Yes, putting women on the wire. In North Carolina, back at the beginning, he dumped them along creeks and rivers. Then he started displaying them. Farm fences in three cases, two chain link fences. But at the same time, DNA matches revealed another favorite pattern, the dumping into a highway ditch."

49

"Are you sure about the rivers?" The agent, a young white man was frowning. "No DNA, no physical evidence. What's the link?"

Deevers said nothing but looked at her laptop on the podium. The display behind her blurred as she jumped to another slide.

"Follow the sequence," she said. North Carolina, a green triangle, appeared. Then the state's rivers appeared. "These are his, no doubt – pattern, DNA." A cluster of red dots appeared, roughly following Interstate 95 but clumped at interstate's intersection with U.S. 64. "Now the river killings…"

Additional red dots appeared following the parallel Tar and Cape Fear Rivers. All of the dots were east of the interstate, though the rivers extended well beyond it to the northwest.

"All start close to his drops off of I-95," she said. "Level of violence is similar. Dates work. One other thing." She paused. "This is the segue I told you I wanted to save for last. Well, here it comes." She took a breath.

"He's been helped," Deevers said. "An agent in North Carolina, working in deep cover as part of an anti-terrorist investigation, provided information on a person of interest whose movements appear to match those of our killer."

"First, the bad news. We don't have a name. Our agent was and is working on an informal network of extremist organizations in the Carolinas. Klan, neo-Nazi, extremist militia. He, our agent, learned of a man with ties to the Aryan Brotherhood's 'Order of the Blood' in North Carolina who had been sent 'up north' after problems arose. While unable to get specific details, it appears the man in question murdered for the chapter but ran into trouble when he committed some unsanctioned killings. This violation of discipline ordinarily would be punished by death but the local Blood people 'traded' him to an organization in Virginia."

"Traded?" the State Trooper detective asked.

"'Traded' was the word, though we don't know what for. We suspect it would have been for the obvious – weapons, money, or drugs. Whatever it was, if it happened that way, the movement north of this person matches our killer's timeline."

"We think, in exchange for his services, the organizations he's been passed to provided cover and income." She turned and gestured at the screen. "Next slide, please."

Black dots joined the red ones though were spread in wider patterns.

"Among these victims," she said, "we have a prosecutor, a state judge wounded, two police officers, one killed, and a number of other people who are sometimes the targets of extremist groups. The cases are in your handout and are coded to the numbers for the dots. They match his timeline. These attacks are different, as you'll read. Generally, gunshot, handgun, two by shotgun, one, a doctor, by large caliber rifle."

"These kills show no significant skill with firearms, by the way. A fair number of people were not killed due to poor shot accuracy, suggesting he was not trained." She took a breath.

"The use of firearms is not what we see in his attacks on women. We have not identified a killing of a woman where he used a gun. Knife, blunt instrument, strangulation, with the majority showing knife involvement even when not the cause of death."

Deevers looked around the room and nodded to someone in back. The lights came on and she turned off the display.

"Our man," she said, "was not with any Order of Blood in Virginia. The 'AB' hasn't gotten a Blood group running there. On the other hand, they are slightly tied in with Nazis and, less so, with some Klan who get weapons from them. Those ties are looser than in the past when the Brotherhood was just a white supremacist gang operating out of prisons. When they partnered up with the Mexican gangs, it was primarily to get an ally in the drug wars rather than protecting the white race. Nowadays, whatever they sell their members, they are simply another organized crime group and the neo-Nazis and Klan generally regard them with contempt as drug-dealing criminals. That includes the Aryan Nation religious people. Still, they talk to one another and our people think our person of interest might be useful to such groups and fit this pattern."

"The other killings, the unsanctioned ones…?"

"Our agent doesn't know," she said. "He hasn't gotten any specific word, so they could be anything, anyone, though we think those unsanctioned ones were the women we've identified in North Carolina. Remember, our guy is pretty deep but he's got other priorities."

"Like staying alive."

"There's that," she said. "But he thinks the word is pretty solid. As for the murders he committed, they seem to be a part of the fight to control drug trafficking and hit various law enforcement people. Our friends in the DEA have identified two they think probably belong to the same hitter and three others that might."

"I notice," the Trooper said, "we don't have a DEA rep on the task force. Is the assumption that he is not affiliated with the drug trade up here?"

"Yes," she said. "While with the Aryan Brotherhood in North Carolina, he did not seem to be involved with drugs – moving them, selling them. He was just there as muscle. In Virginia and Maryland, we haven't picked up on anything suggesting he's involved himself with the drug business there and we're thinking that has remained the pattern here."

"This last killing," the State Trooper said, "yesterday, she was 'personal,' then, not related to doing business for some extremist group?"

"So far," she said, "that's how it looks. This one may have just been for thrills."

Several minutes and a handful of questions later, the meeting broke up. People scattered to various assignments while several remained in the room, reading the report Deevers had prepared.

Dave Barrows, the FBI agent in charge of the task force, walked up to Deevers as she gathered her notes. With him was the State Trooper, a tall, older black man with white grazing his temples.

"Wanted to introduce you two," Barrows said. His hand, in a kid's pistol shape pointed at her. "Karen Deevers, Special Agent from Behavioral Science at Quantico, on loan to us for the duration." The finger-barrel swung to one side. "Phillip Ross, Lieutenant, Major Case Team, Pennsylvania State Police."

"I know Lieutenant Ross already, though indirectly," Deevers said, extending her hand. Ross took it in a firm grip and shook it. "When PACIC caught that pattern, he was one of the signatories to the notification to us."

"The Intelligence Center folks," Ross said, "just wanted the report to be readable and so ran it past me." He smiled. "If I could make sense out of it…"

"Even us Fee-Bees could?" Deevers smiled back. "Don't be so sure of that. The BSU isn't that far from DC."

"Kids," Barrows said, "let's play nicely. Anyway, Phil…"

"Phillip," Ross said. "Everyone calls my father 'Phil' and I look behind me every time someone uses his name."

"Phillip," Barrows said, shaking his head slightly, "is lead for PA."

"Volunteered or drafted?" Deevers asked.

"Neither. They called for volunteers and I turned around and found everyone else had taken a step back." He shrugged and smiled. "So here I am."

Though Barrows' eyebrows went up in alarm, Deevers smiled back.

"Great," she said. "Good to have you with us. I'm heading out to the latest victim site. Can you come with me?"

"Yes," Ross said. "I have task force wheels."

"Great," Deevers said again. She stuffed her papers into a small bag and slid her laptop in next to them. "Let's do it."

A few minutes later, the pair was in a white car and following a gently turning country road west.

"Your forensic people are there," he said, putting his cellphone down.

"Just getting a walk-through," Deevers said. "Your people have been through the area for any material needing collecting or processing. A couple of our forensic people have been to other sites and are looking for anything that will give us a pattern."

"Good idea," he said.

"You were out there this morning," she said. "Anything strike you that isn't going into the paperwork?"

"One thing," Ross said, glancing both ways as he pulled away from a stop sign. "This victim was placed with some unnecessary risk."

"What do you mean?"

"He had to go into the woods with the body," Ross said. "Just a little way beyond was the owner of the property. There wasn't a great chance he would be seen but it was a chance he could have avoided by placing the body a little further away."

"Anything else?"

"He had to know it would be found," he said. "Either by sight or by smell. Again, while the fence he used for his display was old and down in sections, there were parts that were very well concealed and far enough away that someone would have to be walking around in the brush to smell decomposition. He picked one of the few places where it was likely to be noticed."

"How do you interpret all that?"

"He's working hard for the thrill," Ross said. He thought for a moment. "That became clearer to me when I saw all the sites you've identified so far. He's been at it a while and has to escalate to get anything like the old rush." He glanced at her. "How am I doing so far?"

"I agree with everything you've said," Deevers said. "Let me add to it. We think he has deliberately imposed on himself greater challenges, both in terms of victims and what he's done with the bodies. Early on, he dumped them into rivers and creeks."

"North Carolina."

"Right. If he did any before that, we guess he buried them because we haven't found any pre-dating North Carolina that match his later behavior patterns."

"What about victim patterns?"

"Of course, there are missing women, but…"

"There are always missing women."

"Yes. Beyond that, he has not specialized other than by race. All white. Wide variety of occupations, age range of 18 to 38, and so on. We have our suspicions about some of the missing ones, but nothing hard."

"Anyway, as he's moved north, though the killings often differ in technique, they have in common that he has gradually moved to greater exposure."

"When did he start tying them to fences?"

"Just before leaving North Carolina he tried it out. In Virginia he put one in a dumpster but I think that was just a test – what would be the splash when the trash collectors came? But they used a lift truck and didn't see anything. The body wasn't spotted until after it was dropped into the landfill. We figured out the dumpster part from trash that had caught in the wrist wires."

"Has he always used wire?"

"No. First it was rope and tape. He began using wire about half way through his Carolina kills."

"Why? It would take longer to secure the victim than rope or tape."

"Power; it looks more brutal."

"I see." Ross paused. "Anything else you think he's doing to increase the thrill?"

"Besides the placement of the bodies, he's marking the bodies to make sure he gets the credit. Those lightning, zig-zag marks on their thighs, that's pretty regular now. Both the Pennsylvania victims had them."

"Yes," Ross said, "I saw them. They look like neo-Nazi stuff. How much a part of them is he?"

"We are not certain, but our profile suggests he would not be a joiner. Not someone to cooperate. A couple of us think he just likes the double lightning symbols. Power. A profiler I talked with suggested he did it deliberately to steer attention towards the same groups that have been helping him."

"Why? That might put him in greater danger."

"Maybe for that reason, more of a thrill. Also, the profiler thinks he might want to foul his own nest."

"You mean, even though they have helped him, he might want to mess them up?"

"Like I said, not a team player. But, yes. Underneath it all he probably resents them for helping him."

"Sweet guy," Ross said. He fell silent for a moment. "So, we know about the Aryan Brotherhood, neo-Nazi, and Klan outfits that he might have used for cover. Who is he using here?"

"Who do you have?"

"We have the whole range of idiots," Ross said. "We have neos, Klan, white supremacists, black supremacists, skinheads, and more militia groups than you can number. One of the factions of the Aryan Nations was up in Potter County until it went down to South Carolina but we still have some of them around, running their racism through a born-again Christian thing. According to your stats, only a few states have more hate groups than us."

"I've seen the numbers," Deevers said. "Why do you think that's the case?"

"We're an old state," Ross said. "Static, flat-line population. Some of our best young people go elsewhere. Coal, steel, all gone. Cities are staggering; the economy was hard hit even before the Bush recession. A big chunk of the state is still wilderness so there are plenty of places for privacy." He paused. "But that's not all of it." He slowed for another intersection.

"A lot of people," Ross said, "feel like everything is out of control, out of their reach. There are people ready and waiting to hand out a line, 'It's not you, it's them,' whoever the 'them' they want nailed. And a way of distracting away from the real pigs at the trough." He shrugged.

"Sure, the rest of us aid and abet by tearing down what was once the world's finest educational system into something the Taliban would regard as regressive, so people don't have the tools to judge what they're being told. And the media just do the talking heads, he said-she said bull shit without bothering to do the fact-check work and stand up and say, 'Representative, that's a crock.'" He shook his head. "What would Murrow say?"

"You paint," Deevers said, "with a broad brush." She smiled.

"It's just that I figure there's enough guilt to go around," Ross said. He returned the smile. "I don't think it's all fallen off a cliff. There are a lot of good people out there trying to do the right thing. I just need to remind myself of that from time to time."

"Well," she said, "I think you are right about some of that. Let me get back to our perp. If these groups have been passing him around, who in Pennsylvania would be looking for an outside hitter?"

"Well," Ross said, "the obvious, sure. Someone with a hair up their ass about abortion doctors, maybe separatists looking to nail a judge or prosecutor. Not the militia; they are mostly about digging in and getting ready for the day." He paused. "Maybe someone with a hard target, someone they can't get to or find, someone you would need better than local talent. Hell, I don't know. Who did he work with in Maryland?"

"Unknown," she said. "Our guy thinks it was Klan, maybe white separatists. Those two overlap sometimes, at least in membership."

"Not Nazi?"

"We haven't gotten a ripple from CIs working on them, nor has Maryland. They are pretty confident that they have a good bead on those people."

"Well, maybe. But I would guess he would be moving very low, very dark. If you can identify any of the people who actually handled him, I think you would find there were only two or three people in each place who knew he was there and maybe only one who knew why."

"I tend to agree," Deevers said. She glanced at a road marker. "We're getting close?"

"Only in our travels," Ross said, his smile returning.

Chapter 10

The conference room was a little small for all the people in it and several stood against the pale green walls. Everyone had a tablet or a small laptop but their eyes were on the thin woman standing at the head of the table.

Ellen Parker was not what anyone except a lover would call "pretty," but her high cheekbones presented a pair of golden-brown eyes that were alight with intelligence. Her straight nose and thin lips were almost severe but the effect was softened by her easy smile. She pushed her hand through her hair, cut in a style that her cutter assured her looked "pixie with an attitude," whatever the hell that meant. In any case, it was short enough to stay out of the way.

"All right, then," she said, "we'll get the city council stuff in and the other feeds in their usual positions. Council gets the primary headline block," the decision brought a groan from a couple of people at the table, "so nail the picture down from the three we got."

"Not the mayor," one of the groaners said and everyone laughed.

"Not the mayor," Parker agreed. "Four headline blocks below are the police rescue story, use the picture of the officer with the kid, the bridge inspection story, the eroded concrete picture, the Philly trades story with the picture of the new pitcher being told he was going to Philadelphia, I love the chagrin, and, in the last block, the science kids story."

"Which picture?"

"The three firing the laser, but if the size is too small for clarity, use the other one and save the laser for the article page."

Parker was an assistant editor for the Philadelphia Enquirer's online presence, which mostly meant taking the feeds from the print side and pouring them into the web site. Other than a few blogs and occasional specialty items, the web site basically repeated everything that appeared in print.

During the past several years, the process had become steadily more efficient. Now, when a reporter wrote up a story, when the appropriate editor and fact checkers finished with it, the story went in two directions – one to the computer that did the printing of the newspapers and one to the computer that managed the web site. That held for the work in the Daily News, a faintly tabloid newspaper now owned by the Inquirer.

But the web site, Philly.com, did more than that. It was a 24/7 operation that exchanged information and stories with independent news sources both in Philadelphia and from around the world. It seemed to be in a continuous state of updating itself – the staff joked that, if it was in the newspaper, it was history; if it was on the site, it was news.

It was not a joke repeated "on the print side."

"Anything else?" she asked but there was no response; many people were already working on their computers.

Parker nodded and people slipped out of the room. She picked up her computer – she disliked the lack of a real keyboard of most tablets – when she felt her cell phone buzz in her pocked. As she made her way to the door, she put the phone up to her ear.

"Ellen Parker," she said.

"Elizabeth Chernov," a woman said. "Do you have a minute?"

"Hey, Beth," Parker said, stepping through the door another woman held for her. She silently mouthed her thanks. "What's happening?"

"I think I have a problem," Chernov said slowly. "I don't mean the head kind. Maybe I do. I don't know what the fuck is going on but I need to talk to someone I can trust."

"Thanks for the compliment," Parker said as she slipped through the rows of desks – hers had cubicle walls around it defining some space and serving for her neighbors' efforts to pin up their call lists and kids' art work.

She put her laptop on her desk and shook her head negatively to someone holding up some paper. She flashed her fingers and the person nodded. She dropped into her seat. "What's happening?"

"A little girl showed up at the cabin," Chernov said. "Had a story of running away from some shooting. I called a buddy in the police. He said there had been a shooting on the other side of the lake. You know where I'm talking about?"

"I remember. The log cabin place. Mr. Lowenstein's."

"It looks like the bad guys may have followed the girl," Chernov said. If there had been a trace of anxiety in her voice before it was gone now. All Parker heard was the ice-like calm the other woman could turn on when she needed it. "We were pursued but got away."

58

She fell silent and Parker hesitated.

"Are you in touch with the police now?"

"No," Chernov said. "I may be paranoid but I think... It's possible that they figured out where we went because someone in the police told them."

"Are you safe now?"

Chernov laughed.

"Thanks for not asking if I was crazy," she said.

"You're not crazy," Parker said. "Remember, I talked to your shrink."

"Yeah, well, she's not too well wrapped herself. Hell, Ellen, she works for the government."

"Understood," Parker said, smiling slightly. "Back to my question. Are you safe now?"

"Yes," Chernov said. "They seem to have left and we're headed in the opposite direction."

"And you want me to help how?"

"I need to bring this kid in to someone," Chernov said slowly. "But I'm running on 'combat rules' now and I don't know who to trust. I don't know what's going on with the police – maybe everything there is all right, I'm just seeing things. I don't know." She paused. "I need someone who's got their act together to bounce off of and help me get her safe."

Parker noticed that Chernov was focused on the girl's safety, not her own. "Combat rules," a phrase that had come up when Parker wrote an article on women in the service, including taking care of those needing help. To soldiers, the rules were simple: the first was the duty of the strong was to protect the weak.

"All right," she said. "Give me some information. I'm at my desk and will check out what you've got."

"Roger that," Chernov said. "Girl's name is Sharon Stuart."

"Hold on for a sec." Parker's fingers blurred on her keyboard. "Got it. Chester County report. There's been a shooting... This is bad, Beth. Can you talk?"

"Sharon's here," Chernov said. "I'm on my cell."

"It's developing," Parker said, reading her screen. "Two dead, one named 'Stuart,' woman, identified as Margaret Stuart. And a man, David O'Brien. Both shot dead. In the trailer park across the lake from you. No suspects identified. County Sheriff and State Troopers working the case. Next note. Drug lab found." She paused.

"Beth, if she was there…"

"Yeah, I figured." The woman released a long sigh. "This is not good."

"We got to get you to the police," Parker said. She raised her hand and waved it. Two desks away a young man with a goatee looked up and she motioned him over.

"Been there, done that," Chernov said. "I don't know how or why, but cops may be mixed up in this." She paused. "Maybe someone I worked with."

"I may have something," Parker said. As the young man walked up to her, she scrawled a quick note and handed it to him. He looked at it, raised his eyebrows, and then nodded. He quickly returned to his desk.

"I know someone," Parker said. "Squeaky clean. Not local. She's FBI. Let me bring her into this."

Chernov said nothing for a moment and Parker remembered how intense the woman's silences could be. Finally, she spoke again.

"Here's what we do," Chernov said. "You call your FBI friend. Give her my number. I'll arrange for her to come out here and meet us. But I want you there, I want to see at least one face I know. But no one else."

"Got it," Parker said. "Give me few minutes and I'll call you back."

"Understood," Chernov said and the connection broke.

Parker looked up and the young man held up three fingers. She punched in the third button on her desk telephone.

"Ellen Parker," she said.

"Karen Deevers," a woman said. "What can I do for you, Ellen? I'm a bit busy at the moment."

"Hey, got something going on and may need your assistance."

"Assistance?" There was a pause. "As I recall, you're pretty good at taking care of yourself."

"It's not like that," Parker said. "No shooting need be involved. It sounds like there's already been enough."

"What's going on?"

"Got called by a woman named Elizabeth Chernov," Parker said. "She's got a girl with her named Sharon Stuart. Apparently, the girl's mother and a man were killed earlier today and the girl escaped. Beth thinks they are being pursued by the bad guys, though she seems to have shaken them off."

"Tell her to go to the nearest police."

"She said she tried to do that and the bad guys almost got them. She's an ex-cop and she's thinking the locals may be working with them, maybe even someone from her old department."

Deevers was silent for a second.

"Who is Chernov?"

"I interviewed her for a series we did on service women in Iraq and Afghanistan. She's Pennsylvania National Guard, did two deployments. She was a police officer in the New Joyton Police Department for nine years."

"I'll read the article," Deevers said. "She reliable?"

"When I talked to her ten months ago," Parker said, "she was clean. She'd had a problem with alcohol after she got back."

"PTSD?"

"Yes. Some combat stuff and a sexual assault. Her therapist, who she gave me permission to interview, said she was in good shape."

"All right," Deevers said. "I've got the article up. Says you got a Pulitzer nomination. Congratulations."

"Thanks," Parker said. "Didn't get anything for my 'Women in Law Enforcement' story, though."

"Poor subject matter. Looks like they really messed with her after the rape. And she had more than 'some' combat. Those runs into the Green Zone from the airport in the old days must have been like being in Deadwood. Silver Star, not bad for an MP. You got a number for me?"

"Yes," Parker said and paused. "She wants me with you. Familiar face."

"Lovely," Deevers said, her voice indicating the situation was anything but lovely. "I'll give you time to talk to her. Then I'll call at... Let's make it half past. Here's the thing. I am butt deep in alligators just now, so ask her to be punctual."

"Got it, thanks."

"No problem. See you soon."

Parker used her cell phone to call Chernov.

"Do you trust her?" was Chernov's question.

"Yeah, I do."

"Why?"

"I know her, did an article." Parker paused. "We go back to when I was a kid in Ohio. She helped bring down the gang that killed my cousin. Then, here..."

"I read about that. She was the Deevers in your article. She sounds all right."

"I didn't know you read that."

"I was bored and there wasn't anything on YouTube. I'll wait for her call."

"Cool. She agreed I could be there."

"Still trying for the Pulitzer, huh?"

"Somebody's got to win one."

"And the lottery, too. All right, talk to you later."

"'Bye."

"So now we wait," Chernov said.

"I need a bathroom," the little girl said.

"Of course. You hungry, too?"

"I don't want to eat. You can if you want to."

"No, I don't have much of an appetite." She nodded down the road. "Hey, that pizza place looks clean. We'll give their restroom a try."

"Get a pizza?"

"I thought," Chernov said as she turned in past a sign that read "Little Anthony's," "you weren't hungry."

"You started talking about food."

Chernov smiled and parked in front of the white building but all the way at the end, trying to stay out of sight of the highway.

The place was clean and Chernov walked Sharon to the restroom. She stepped over to the counter and studied the pizzas on display.

"Just out," one of the people behind the counter said and motioned to a pizza. He had a thick, black mustache. He turned to another man and talked quickly in what sounded like Arabic.

Chernov pursed her lips for a second and then, as she looked around, her heart beating a little more firmly than it had, she saw a picture on the wall of a bunch of men with black mustaches in suits standing together behind a tall, teenage girl wearing a robe. The man saw her looking.

"Mike's girl," he said. "We all went to graduation."

"She looks pretty."

The man's smile widened.

"She's got straight A's," he said. "She's gonna be a doctor."

"That's great," she said. "Let me have four slices of the chicken and broccoli."

"You got it," he said. "What are you drinking?"

"Couple of cokes, please."

"You got it. Have a seat, I bring it to you."

"Thanks."

"Call me Sam."

"Thanks, Sam. Call me Beth."

"You got it, Beth."

Chernov found a booth where she could see the entrance and the windows facing the highway. She listened to the men behind the counter – it was Arabic but she didn't hear any words she remembered – and glanced in the direction of the restrooms just as Sharon came out.

"I'm hungry," she said as she slid into a seat.

Before Chernov could reply, her phone buzzed. She glanced at the display but the number was blocked.

"Hello," she said.

"Elizabeth? Agent Karen Deevers. Ellen Parker called me. What's going on?"

"I'm with Sharon, Sharon Stuart." She paused. "She came to me on the run."

"I understand," Deevers said. "I'm aware of the situation. You don't think you can go to the local police?"

"No, not really." She paused again. "I did that and the people showed up."

"Understood. All right, where are you?"

"322, just east of Honey Brook, north side of the highway. A place called 'Little Anthony's'."

"Got it. I'm not very far from you. OK, here's the thing. I'm working a case. I'll probably be twenty-five, thirty minutes before I break free and then another fifteen or twenty before I get to you. Is that all right?"

"It'll have to be."

"I'll let Ellen Parker know we've talked and suggest she go directly to you. I'm guessing she'll get there before me or a little after. Is that all right?"

"As I said."

"I hear you. Listen, I will be there. Don't move. We don't want to play telephone tag."

"All right. See you when you get here."

"Depend on it."

Chernov looked at her phone and frowned; the battery indicator was very low and she didn't have a recharger. She shrugged and put it away. The FBI agent's suggestion to avoid phone tag was a good one.

"What's going on?" Sharon asked.

"I have a friend coming," Chernov said, "and she has a friend who's coming, too." She tried to smile. "We won't bother to save them any pizza."

"I will."

"You're a nice person," Chernov said.

"Ellen Parker."

"Hey, it's Karen. Talked to Chernov. She sounds pretty spooky. Anyway, I'm aware of the shooting – the little girl with her is the child of one of the victims. I've got to finish a few things here and then I'll go to her. In the meantime, how about you go there now? I'm hoping to get there about the same time you do. 322, Little Anthony's outside Honey Brook."

"Sounds like a plan," Ellen said. She waved at the coworker with the goatee again. "I'll GPS it. I'm going now."

"Good. See you there."

"Right, 'bye." Ellen turned to the man. "Hey, got to run, if anyone looks for me. May have part of the story about those shootings at the trailer park."

"I'll pass the word," he said. "That thing has lit up everything. Will you be checking in?"

"Just as soon as I find out what the deal is." She stood and grabbed her bag and a light jacket draped over her chair.

"You'll need your cell," he said, raising his eyebrows and pointing at her desk.

"I have a mind like a steel trap," she said, grabbing the phone.

"Hard and rusty?" he asked.

"Ha. Ha. See you later."

As Deevers put away her phone, she explained the situation to Ross. The forensics people, two from the FBI, one to conduct the tour from the State Police, all stood a little distance away and acted like they weren't listening to the conversation between the two.

"She thinks someone is rotten in her old department?"

"That was Parker's impression."

"Maybe a little paranoid?"

"Aren't we all?"

Ross laughed. "Is she dug in somewhere?"

"Pizza place outside of Honey Brook, Little Anthony's."

"I know it," Ross said. "Nice place. Jordanian family runs it. Got another place with the same name over in Thorndale."

"Is there anything the Pennsylvania State Troopers don't know?"

Ross laughed again.

"Am I coming?" he asked.

"Better if I go alone," Deevers said. "I'll need to take the car. Can you get one of the techs to give you a ride?"

"Not a problem," he said. "One of the guys down at the shooting can swing up here and pick me up on his way to his barracks." He took out his cell phone and called the dispatcher. He took a moment to walk part of the crime scene with Deevers. As she stopped to examine the fence, he punched in the cell number of a State Trooper at the trailer park.

"Trooper Kindle," a woman answered. Ross grimaced. So much for 'one of the guys' and he wondered if he was ever going to get out of the habit of using the masculine when referring to his fellow troopers. And was 'fellow' all right?

"Phillip Ross," he said.

"Dispatcher already called me, sir," she said. "You need a ride?"

"If you can get away," he said. "I need to return to base."

"Not a problem, sir. The Deputies are wrapping up here and the leads have released us."

"Me, too," Ross said. "My Fee-Bee buddy is going over to a place on 322 near Honey Brook and it's too far to the nearest bus stop."

"Ain't one where you are, sir. I'm on my way."

"Thanks, trooper."

Trooper Ann Kindle waved to one of the county deputies and started walking to her car.

"Got to go," she said. "Taxi service for the task force."

"Whoa," the Deputy said. "You're getting into the big leagues." He grinned; he had been trying to get a conversation going with Kindle ever since she had arrived.

Kindle laughed, a short bark.

"Hardly," she said as she reached her car and took off her campaign hat. "The feds dumped him and took off for Honey Brook. Some place on 322."

"Be safe," the Deputy said.

Kindle nodded and carefully backed out of the small group of police cruisers gathered at the trailer park entrance. A moment later, she was speeding through the late afternoon light.

"Damn," the Deputy said.

"What's wrong?"

The Deputy turned and faced one of the town cops that had been in and out all day.

"Missed my chance," the Deputy said. "She had to go give someone a ride so she's off to Honey Brook and the path of true love comes to an abrupt halt."

"'True love,' huh?" Sergeant Don Brunner said. He shook his head. "Staties, man, they're always on the move. Next year she could be somewhere on the Ohio line." He looked around. "Well, it doesn't look like you guys need any other help from me."

The Deputy nodded; sometimes the locals assisted with traffic and such but Brunner had wandered around the area as if he was playing detective. No loss when he left.

"Got it," Jacks said. He looked at the driver. "Turn around. They didn't go to Downingtown. Maybe back up at Honey Brook."

"Hot damn," the driver said. He pulled out of the gas station parking lot that gave them a good view of the intersection of US routes 30 and 322.

Books felt his heart soar – there was no other word for it. His chance he thought he had lost was his again. He settled back into his seat and grinned. He still had a chance to prove himself, to become valued. And he knew what it would take.

Two in the head.

Chapter 11

By the time they got home, Taylor had melted, the grief seeming to steal her muscles and bones, dissolving who she was and turning her into someone with nothing except the grief. JJ got her into her apartment, stayed for a short period of time to help her make phone calls, and then withdrew.

He heated up some leftovers for an early dinner and used them as an excuse to check in on her.

Taylor, her eyes red, sat with her phone open on the coffee table in front of her, and looked at him as if he was someone on the other side of a divide. She was in a land that most all explored, he knew, and, somehow, he believed that she would find her way back.

"Got some food downstairs," JJ said. "Want to eat something?"

She shook her head.

"I've called everyone I'm supposed to," she said. "I don't think I could tell anyone else what happened."

"Take a break," JJ said. "Unless there's someone you want to talk to…"

"No one," she said. "Not tonight."

"OK, why not put away your phone? Give yourself a chance to unwind a little."

"Her brother gets in tonight. We talked. He's got a friend who will pick him up at the airport. He told me to take care of myself." Her red eyes stared at him from the other side of the divide. "How do I do that now?"

"Gently," JJ said. He waited to see if she heard that.

She said nothing for a moment and then reached out to the phone. It went dark.

"I don't know if I can eat," she said, "but let me get out of this apartment."

"Come with me," he said.

When they got to his apartment, her lips went tight and she shook her head. "No food."

He made sure the microwave was off and motioned with his head to the back deck. She followed as if walking meant something.

A few minutes later, they were in chairs, staring into the shadows of late afternoon. An untouched beer was on the table beside her and he sipped at his diet soda mechanically.

"This thing," she said. "This thing has happened before."

"Maybe, I don't know."

"I would like to know what really happened."

He nodded.

"Do you think Karen would know?" she asked. "Could she find out? I don't think any of the locals are going to tell me anything."

"I don't know." It was the only thing he could think to say.

"Would you mind calling her?" She blinked hard and made a tight smile. "I know that's asking a lot, with everything going on with you two, but could you?"

JJ felt his heart beat. He had been saying he would call Karen but…

"All right," he said. "I'll call her first thing in the morning. I don't know if she can find out anything. I don't even know what her current assignment is but I'll ask."

"Thank you, JJ."

The two of them remained on the deck until dark settled comfortably over the West Branch of the Brandywine and well after people died on the road to Honey Brook.

As much as Books wanted the driver to floor it, he understood Jacks' instructions were the right ones. Stay within the speed limit, slow down when passing anything looking like a restaurant or store so everyone could check the parking lot for that piece of shit Honda, and, above all, keep the weapons out of sight.

"Maybe thirteen miles," the driver said. "Depending on traffic, probably take us twenty minutes."

"They turned north from that restaurant," Jacks said. "You can put some speed on until we reach it. After that, remember what I said."

The driver nodded and the SUV surged forward.

Books scanned every parking lot they passed, including the ones before the restaurant where they missed their targets. He was eager to find them but did not want to make a mistake. He looked even when there was little likelihood of seeing them.

They were more than a mile outside of Honey Brook when he saw a hatchback red Honda, sitting in the furthest parking space of a pizza place called Little Anthony's.

The pizza was good and Chernov discovered she had an appetite. Sharon was quiet which she thought was to be expected. Sometimes when things went insane, adults would run in circles but the kids would hold in place, silent, trying to digest it.

There was this time in Iraq… She pulled herself away from the memory.

"We left my backpack in the car," Sharon said, looking up, holding a slice of pizza with both hands. She looked around. "Is it safe there?"

"Probably," Chernov said and then tried to remember if she had locked the doors. She could not remember doing it. Finally, she sighed and put her soda down.

"Just to be safe," she said, "I'm going to go get your backpack so we can keep an eye on it."

Sharon nodded in an adult fashion and didn't bother to watch Chernov get up and leave.

Chernov walked outside and noticed the light was noticeably dimmer. She turned to her left and followed the wall to the end of the parking lot. She walked up to the Honda; she had backed it into a slot, so she reached the passenger door. She pulled on it and, frowning, found it was unlocked.

Stupid.

She reached behind the seat and picked up the backpack. She tripped the switch to lock all the doors and heard them all give a solid mechanical click. Chernov stood and stopped herself from closing the door. It wasn't a good idea to leave a handgun in a car – if someone stole the car, she would have armed a criminal. She reached into the glove compartment and took out the .45 and its clip, stuffing both into the bag. She zipped up the bag as she walked back to the entrance.

Sharon was still eating as Chernov sat down and put the pack on the floor between her feet.

"You seem to be enjoying that," she said.

"I like broccoli," Sharon said. "It's good for you."

"I've heard that." Chernov looked up as the door opened.

The driver had not slammed on the brakes when Books spotted the Honda. With all the traffic, someone would probably have plowed into their rear. Instead, he kept his speed up until he could pull off into a garage's parking area.

"Are you sure?" Jacks asked Books.

"Only that it was a red hatchback," Books said.

"Right, it could be anyone," Jacks said, nodding. "But we'll check it out." He looked around as the SUV stopped. "All right, here's the deal. We want to get them as they come out, preferably when they get to their car. If it's them, that is. The little girl knows you," he said to the driver, "so Books is going to go in and see if he sees a woman alone with a little girl."

Books nodded, his excitement growing.

"I think if we park there," Jacks said, "they'll recognize us. Maybe call for cops again or something."

"There's a cross-street," the driver said. His fingers tapped at the GPS display. "It's called Cupola. We could go down it and wait with the car. There's a Turkey Hill across the highway and a little way down. Pull in there and wait." He shook his head. "I saw some kind of storage place across the highway from Cupola but I don't think we can park there without attracting attention.

"Turn around and park at the Turkey Hill," Jacks said. The SUV rolled forward and he turned back to Books. "Get moving as soon as we stop."

"Got it," Books said.

"You got your cell," Jacks said as the driver waited for a break in the traffic. "If you see a woman and girl, just call and say something. Then buy a bottle of soda or something and go back outside. Don't look at them. Go out back where the car is. Take a position. Jonesy and I will come over and set up with you; driver stays with the car. We'll take them as they get to the car. As soon as he hears shots, he'll bring the car for us."

"Traffic is getting thick," the driver said. He shook his head. "It's going to be tough to get to you all quickly."

Jacks looked at the cars and trucks. It was clear they were getting into the heavy part of rush hour. Finally, he nodded.

"All right," he said. "Change in plan. Fuck the Turkey Hill. We go down to the street and turn into it. We park in the lot and then everything is as I said. Books in, IDs the two, gets out of there, the three of us wait, shooting starts and the Chevy comes up to take us away. Questions?"

There were none. It was several more minutes before an opening came and the driver dashed into the middle turning lane, found a gap in the east bound traffic, and muscled his way in. A moment later he was back in the turning lane, waiting for the oncoming traffic to give him a hole to turn through.

There was no one on Cupola but the cross traffic was steady.

"No hurry," Jacks said, totally calm and Books admired the man. The red Honda was in plain sight and he knew they had them.

Finally, a gap appeared. The driver lanced through it and then slowed down. He turned in quickly, not wanting to park at the far end where the Honda sat.

"Beautiful," Jacks said. "Not many people in the lot. All right, Books, you're on."

"Got it," Books said.

He was out of the SUV in a smooth movement, totally focused on the front door. He glanced at the door, but he could not clearly see through it any of the customers. Books stepped into the restaurant and immediately the man behind the counter to his right asked him if he wanted anything.

"Just a coke," he said, trying to look around without appearing to look around. "I'll get one from the case."

The man nodded and went back to cutting pizza. Books walked over to the case and saw a couple with a pair of kids and some guy in a motorcycle jacket. He took a bottle out randomly and slowly turned around, trying to delay leaving.

As he stepped up to the cash register, he saw a woman with a child but another woman walked over to them and sat down. The kid stared at him blankly. But two women? He put his money down, trying to figure out what was happening. Finally, he decided there was nothing to be done except to tell Jacks.

Feeling like he had failed in some way, Books walked back to the SUV and climbed in.

"What's the deal?" Jacks asked.

"Saw two kids with a couple," Books said. "Don't think either of the them are right, too young. Saw one kid of the right age but there are two women with her, so I don't know."

Jacks said nothing for a moment, then he nodded.

"All right, maybe they're in the john or something. We wait a little. The right ones come out, we do our thing and we're out of here. If they don't come out quick, driver goes in and says yea or nay."

"Yeah, but..." the driver started to say.

"I know," Jacks said. "The girl might recognize you. Jonesy and I will be right behind you. If she does, we come in. Books, you wait – they might get nervous seeing you come in again. If it is the girl but she doesn't see the driver, we all quietly back out and wait here. Everyone clear?"

Books nodded, disappointed. Damn, he had been so close...

Chernov raised a hand and Ellen Parker walked over and sat down. Chernov didn't notice that Sherrie, her eyes wide, was slowly turning back from staring at the closing restaurant door.

"Good to see you," Parker said.

"Bad penny," Chernov said. She nodded at the little girl. "This is Sharon Stuart. Her friends call her Sherrie. Sherrie, this is Ellen Parker. She works for a newspaper."

"That was him," the girl said.

"What?"

"One of the men at the trailer." Her eyes remained wide.

"Are you sure?" Parker asked.

"Where's my bag? It's in my bag. My phone, it's in my bag." She seemed close to losing control, her voice almost choked, her speech speeding past.

Chernov pulled the bag up to the table and Sherrie pulled at a side pocket, fumbling with a zipper for a second before pulling free a silver camera phone.

Chernov dropped the bag into her lap while Sherrie messed with the camera's controls. She did something with the display and then pointed at a blurry image.

"See? That's him."

"Sherrie," Parker said, "it's hard to make out that man's face. He could be almost..."

"To hell with that," Chernov said, sliding out of her seat. Parker heard something slide shut from within the bag and knew immediately it was a gun. "Sherrie, you're with me. We're using the back door."

"Wait," Parker said, slightly raising her hands. "Deevers will be here in a moment and..."

Then time ran out.

The driver stepped through the door and was greeted by the man behind the glass-enclosed counter. He looked to the right and only then looked to his left. He saw a woman half out of a booth, holding a blue backpack, *the* blue backpack, and the back of a little girl's head. Next to the child another woman had her back to him and was only starting to turn her head. They were leaving.

"Shit," he said, and reached for the pistol in his waistband.

The first woman moved with a swift, smooth motion, as if what she was doing was something that she practiced every day. Her hand came out of the backpack and her narrowed eyes were as hard as the metal of the large handgun in her hand.

"Sherrie, down!" Chernov yelled and Parker saw her raise a dark handgun with both hands. Parker pulled Sherrie to her and down, trying to get underneath the table.

The gun fired, loud enough to set Parker's ears ringing. There was a clink of thin, bouncing metal and then the gun fired again.

Karen Deevers pulled in beside a nondescript red Honda hatchback and took a moment to identify her location to the dispatcher. Then she opened her door. She saw two men outside the pizza place, looking toward the door as if waiting for someone. She smiled to herself; there was always someone who was the last to leave.

She heard two distinct shots, followed by a third, and had her pistol free with the second shot. The two men ignored her, fixated on the front door, and both pulled guns out.

"Federal agent," she yelled, her hands coming up in front of her. There was no time to say anything else.

One of the men turned, almost spun, towards her with a liquid grace, so smooth in his motion he seemed totally relaxed. Part of Deevers' brain identified that one as the dangerous one and she fired.

The man flinched but fired and Deevers felt her side burn. She fired again and then aimed at the second man. As the first collapsed, the second man pointed his gun at her with one hand. He fired but his shot seemed impulsive. Deevers fired and the man fell forward, his body curling and his gun bouncing off the asphalt.

Deevers moved her gun back and forth, pointing at both men, while her side hurt more as she stood there. Finally, she slowly walked forward.

73

The first man, the smooth one, lay on his side, his eyes staring at nothing, while blood spread its stain from his clothes to the parking lot. She walked up to him and used her foot to slide his handgun away from his hand. He did not move.

The second man clutched at his torso, his hands bloody and his eyes closed tightly.

The pain in Deevers' side was getting worse but she had heard shots fired from within the restaurant. She squatted down and picked up the second man's gun and slipped it into her jacket pocket.

"Don't move," she said but the man showed no sign of hearing her. She added the first man's gun to her collection and, her gun extended in front of her, entered the restaurant.

A man lay on his face, arms to either side, while blood pooled from his upper chest and neck. She saw no other threat with a quick scan and crouched beside the man. He had no pulse but she picked up his gun as well.

She saw Ellen Parker half out of the booth and then on her feet, coming towards her. Her eyes were wide.

"It's all right," Deevers said. "I just got scratched." Then she dropped to her knees with Parker sliding beside her.

"We need clean towels," Parker said to the man at the counter, who seemed stunned. "Hurry," she said and the man broke out of his shock. He came around the counter and handed a handful of neatly folded towels to her. He looked at the man and his blood and Deevers, his eyes wide.

"I'm all right," Deevers said. She gasped. "Two outside."

Parked pressed the folded towels against her side.

"Can you hold those in place?"

"Absolutely," Deevers said, swaying slightly. She bit her lower lip. "Where's the girl and your friend?"

"No idea," Parker said. She pulled a cell phone from her pocket and Deevers heard her punch in three digits.

"Dispatcher, my name is Ellen Parker," she said. "We have an officer wounded at Little Anthony's on 322, just east of Honey Brook. We have three perpetrators down, at least one appears dead; I don't know about the others. I am treating the officer's wound. Do you copy?" Parker waited a moment, the cell phone pinned between her shoulder and chin. "Good. I am going off the line to check on two of the perpetrators."

Parker lowered Deevers and looked at the counterman standing over her. He was standing very still, his eyes on the dead man.

"What's your name?" she asked.

"Sam."

"Sam," she said, deliberately using the man's name, "I need you to press this towel against her side. Can you do that?"

"Sure," Sam said. Hearing his name seemed to have brought him out of his trance, though his eyes were still wide. He knelt beside the wounded woman and carefully covered the towels with his hands. "You gonna be OK," he said, nodding to her and giving a tight smile.

Parker took Deever's gun out of her weak hands.

"Don't…"

"Got to be sure," Parker said and patted her shoulder. Then she was gone.

Trooper Kindle heard the call and whipped the car into a savage turn.

"Officer down," she said and Phillip Ross nodded, a little startled at the sudden turn, the drowsiness vanishing.

"Where?"

"Little Anthony's on 322. We'll be there in fifteen."

"Oh, no."

The car's siren came on and it accelerated.

"Dispatcher, this is Ellen Parker. We have a federal agent down, wounded. Two perps are down, dead. One is badly wounded and is not responsive." Parker listened to the dispatcher for a moment and nodded. "I understand. I will keep my phone open." She leaned forward.

"Hey, Karen, it's me." Deevers' eyes opened and then winced. "You got hit in the side, looks to be just under your ribcage. It's a through and through, small hole, not very dramatic."

"Asshole," Deevers said. She swallowed. "I think I'm shocky."

"No big moves," Parker said. "I think we've stopped the bleeding but you lost some before that. Your gun is beside you." She looked up towards the door. "I think the cavalry is here."

"Where's Chernov?" she asked again.

She did not hear an answer.

Chapter 12

Books heard firing from within the pizza place and instinctively pulled out his gun. But Jacks and Jonesy did not move to enter; they paused, leaning forward slightly, as if listening.

He heard a woman shout something and then, incredibly, Jacks went down and then, not so incredibly, so did Jonesy. Books saw a woman, gun pointed, quickly check Jacks and Jonesy and then she was gone into the restaurant.

For a moment, Books froze. What had happened? When he began moving again, it was to get out of the SUV and immediately re-enter it in the driver's position. His hand felt the dangling keys as if moving by itself and a moment later he was on 322, driving away.

It took him several minutes to wonder where he was driving. Then he picked his cellphone out of his pocket and punched in the number for Mr. Tallman.

Something had to be done.

Police of various departments seemed to be a waterfall of black and blue and gray, rapidly filling the restaurant. Close to them were paramedics, adding a shade of light blue to the color array, and they established a line into Karen Deevers at the same time Phillip Ross arrived.

A county Deputy Sheriff saw him and stepped over and then stepped to one side as Deevers was wheeled out on a gurney, followed closely by a thin woman.

"Here's what we got," the deputy said. "Agent Deevers was here to meet a reporter and a woman with the kid from the shooting at the lake."

"I know about that part of it."

"Right. This one," he nodded at the dead man on the floor, "opened fire, or tried to. The woman with the kid, her name is Elizabeth Chernov, put him down. We know her, she's a New Joyton officer on sick leave or something. We got several witnesses on this. Special Agent Deevers was just about to enter the place when two white males started to go in with drawn guns. She challenged them and they turned on her. She put both down. One's dead. The other's in very bad shape and they are moving him down Cupola for a medevac; they are going to put Deevers on the same bird. Church parking lot."

"How bad...?"

"Medic gave me a 'thumbs up' and she was semi-conscious and responsive. She's going to Brandywine. We notified the Sheriff who notified your task force. They are scrambling to get some agents here."

"All right." He looked around. "Where's the woman and child?"

"We don't know," the deputy said. "The other woman, her name is Ellen Parker, said she pulled the girl down and when she got up, she went to Deevers and then checked outside. The other witnesses were on the floor and didn't see them leave the restaurant. But a man thinks he saw a red Honda leave the parking lot and that matches the car registered to Chernov. We've checked for the car but it's gone.'"

"Speaking of cars..."

"APB is out for the perp's car. Deevers and Parker, the reporter who went outside, believe it is a large SUV, dark blue or black. We've also got one out for a red Honda – Deevers saw that one on her way in."

"She was in good enough shape to report the cars."

"Yes, sir," the deputy said, "but groggy." He paused while a siren wailed. "We are talking to everyone here and are holding onto Ellen Parker. Some kind of reporter." He paused again. "I understand this is not on the task force radar."

"No," Ross said. He shook his head. "This is that local shooting down at the lake."

"Parker said the same. Well, we've secured the scene, both in and out, and are waiting for your detectives; Honey Brook's only got a chief and four officers."

"I understand," Ross said. "The Fee-Bees will be involved. I'm going to talk to the task force and see what I can do about keeping the crowd down."

"Good luck on that."

Ross nodded and walked outside, careful where he put his feet. He was a little surprised that the daylight was disappearing. As he took out his phone, he held up a finger indicating he needed a moment and Trooper Kindle nodded.

"Ross here," he said to the task force dispatcher.

"Hold on for Agent Barrows."

"Barrows here. What's happening?"

Quickly Ross explained the situation.

"She's going to be all right?"

"Appears so," Ross said. As he said those words, he felt like he had just exhaled. "She's at Brandywine, or will be in the next few minutes." Somewhere nearby he heard a helicopter. He stuck a finger in his free ear. "I think they may be going now."

"I'll be there. Can you meet me?"

"I'm on my way."

"Good. Tell your people there we have an evidence response team on the way. Philadelphia office is sending people now for your site and the hospital. There's going to be an Investigative Division team up from DC – they are moving now. Federal liaison is being coordinated by Philly for both the Chester County Sheriffs Service and your people. They, in turn, will be calling locals on-scene shortly. This is a federal agent shooting and our protocols are kicking in. Understand?"

"Got it," he said. "Don't worry about those issues. This is an 'officer down.' Everyone here will be coming hard on it."

"See you there."

As Ross finished, Trooper Kindle waved for his attention. He hurried over.

"Sir, we've got people inbound. Can you take a call?"

Ross nodded and in a moment was talking to one of the state police investigators. Quickly he filled the man in, including the remarks from Barrows.

"I understand. I'd feel the same way. We already got the word. The first wave will be from Philly but there are DC people coming, too. Are you headed for the hospital?"

"Affirmative," Ross said. "She's supposed to be all right but…"

"Understood, fingers crossed. We have a sergeant from Embreeville Barracks there hoping to talk to her before surgery, see if it was just those three or any others."

"Got it." He paused and looked around. "I'm going to have people check around for any empty vehicles."

"Good idea. Hold on, just got this. OK, the lead FBI on-scene guy is Special Agent Dwight Monihan. He's coming from Philly. I'm going to be calling down the chain of command there but, if you get the chance, please let the local senior officer present know and gently remind him or her that the

Pennsylvania State Police wish to maintain excellent working relations with our friends in the FBI."

"I think I can do that," Ross said, smiling briefly. "Shall we serve them scrapple?"

"God, no. Let me know how she's doing."

Ross hung up. He found a county deputy and a state trooper and passed on the information he had. Both men nodded.

"One other thing," Ross said. "You might want to check out cars in the area, see if any are unclaimed. Those three dicks got here somehow and may not have used that SUV Deevers saw. Start tracing but don't force entry. The feds will have people who can do that but we may save them some time if we can identify their transportation."

A moment later, lights flashing but siren off, Kindle had them racing down 322.

"We'll go south on 82 and then pick up Reeceville Road," Kindle said but Ross only nodded.

He was trying to remember. Deevers never talked about her personal life but there was something someone said about a husband or something. Ross used his cell phone and called the task force. It was a moment before anyone answered.

"Ross here," he said. "Who is Deevers' next of kin?"

"Already got it. Has a husband, named James J. Jeffers. Listed as an attorney. He's not too far from the hospital. Agent Barrows already called him and he is in transit to Brandywine."

"Understood, thanks. I'll be at Brandywine."

"We got you logged to there, sir."

Ross hung up and watched the scattered houses and farms stream by as darkness layered itself beneath a sky that seemed brighter than the earth.

Deevers had a husband? That was something most cops Ross knew made a point of slipping into a conversation "to avoid complications," to use a common phrase. But Deevers hadn't said anything.

None of his business, of course, but he wondered if Deevers' life was about to become more complicated than a gunshot wound might make it.

Taylor had just gotten to her feet, determined to try to eat something, when JJ's cell buzzed. He grimaced at it and put it to his ear and Taylor smiled sympathetically at him.

79

"Yes, I'm James Jeffers," he said. Then she saw him suddenly bend forward in his chair, as if going into a crouch. "Are you sure? She's here?" He was silent for a moment and Taylor saw his free hand was clenched in a fist. "Are you sure about that, that she's OK?" There was more silence and Taylor felt a wave of awfulness sweep up through her. Karen…

Jeffers stood, the phone still pressed to his ear. His voice was suddenly calm, terribly neutral, and she remembered he had been a police officer.

"I'm fifteen minutes away," he said. He paused while the speaker said something. "Right. Thank you." The cell phone was folded and in his pocket as he walked off the back of the deck.

"Karen's been shot," he said. Taylor hurried to keep up. "She's being brought to Brandywine. They think her wound is minor. It's a 'T-n-T'." He looked at Taylor and she had the sudden thought he'd been talking to himself.

"I'm coming," she said.

He said nothing but his car sprayed gravel as they left the parking area. A moment later, they crossed the West Branch of the Brandywine River heading north. JJ obviously knew how to drive but some of the curves of the country roads leading to Coatesville and Brandywine Hospital beyond were pretty tight.

"JJ," Taylor said, but nothing else.

JJ, his expression hard to see in the car, slowed down slightly, took a breath, and then said, "Sorry."

"No problem."

The hospital emergency room was at the far end of the hospital and the drive to it seemed to take longer than the sprint had. JJ and Taylor hurried to the doors and entered.

The room was surprisingly quiet, though a state trooper stood beside the doors in the back of the ER.

JJ had his identification out as he approached the barrier of Plexiglas that protected the clerk.

"My name is James Jeffers," he said, showing his driver's license. "I am the husband of Karen Deevers."

"Sir, may I?" asked a gravelly voice from beside the doors to the ER's inner sanctum. He reached for JJ's identification, examined it, and compared it to a folded sheet of paper from his pocket. He handed it back.

"Sir," the state trooper said, "your wife went into surgery just a few minutes ago. I talked with her very briefly. They're pretty busy up there with her and the other one, can I help you?"

"How is she?" JJ asked. Before the trooper, an older man with a touch of white in his short hair, could respond, he added, "I'm a former county deputy sheriff, nine years on the job. Please tell me what you know."

The trooper said nothing for several seconds, studying JJ.

"All right," he said. "She seemed in good shape and the docs think she'll be fine. She was wounded. It was a through and through, middle right side. Preliminary X-ray showed no frags, no bone chips, missed the liver, the doc said, but might have nicked the kidney. That's pretty much all I know except her boss, FBI Special Agent Barrows, is on the way."

"Did they give you a time estimate for the surgery?"

"No, sir," the trooper said. "Why don't you check in with the clerk so they'll know to grab you when they get anything specific?"

"Good idea. Thank you," JJ said. The trooper nodded.

JJ talked with the clerk who checked his name on a form sent from the Philadelphia FBI office, apparently not trusting the best efforts of the state trooper. She told JJ as soon as they knew anything, they'd tell him.

Just as JJ sat down, men swarmed into the room. All were cops, JJ figured, because they went to the trooper first. Unflappable, the trooper passed on whatever news he had and always ended his presentation with a nod in JJ's direction. Rather than sit down, the police officers – all were in plain clothes – stood around, murmuring to one another.

A woman emerged clad in a white doctor's coat and he stood but she was intercepted by the officers. The doctor turned and led the way through the doors and two men followed her. JJ saw concern on her face and walked forward.

"Mr. Jeffers?" A man in a suit reached into his coat pocket and brought out his FBI identification. "I'm Special Agent Dave Barrows." He flipped the ID closed. "I understand the trooper filled you in on your wife's condition."

"Yes, he did."

Barrows' eyes went past Jeffers and touched on Taylor, standing next to the chairs. His eyes widened slightly with surprise.

"Excuse me, Mr. Jeffers, but is that Aretha Taylor?"

"Yes, it is. She's a friend. What happened to my wife?"

"We are still determining that," Barrows said. "Your wife…" He frowned slightly. "Are you aware of an apparent drug-related shooting earlier today?"

"West side of the county?" JJ nodded, feeling confused.

"What happened was your wife was asked to meet with a woman who had one of the survivors of that shooting, a young girl. While going to the meeting, a shooting took place. Two are dead, your wife and one other were wounded."

"Who asked her?"

"A reporter, a woman named Ellen Parker."

For a moment, JJ stood perfectly still, long enough for Barrows to frown. "Mr. Jeffers?"

"This Ellen Parker," JJ said. "By any chance, is she from Ohio?"

The red Honda left Little Anthony's as if the driver had nothing more on her mind than getting a medium double cheese home without causing the cheese to slide to one side. She turned north onto 322, drove a mile, and then turned right. Chernov stopped after several hundred yards, pulling off onto a wide shoulder designed to accommodate Amish buggies.

She sat very still, her hands gripping the steering wheel tightly, her eyes straight ahead, as if there was something on the darkening lane that she needed to see.

"What the hell?" she asked. If there was a reply, she did not hear it, for she repeated the question before finally throwing open the door and getting out of the car. Her head down, she looked as if she studied the shoulder as she paced out to the limit of the headlights.

Sharon watched, so terrified that she did not move, fearful that the slightest movement would make everything worse. It was not the shooting in Little Anthony's that had frozen her; pinned beneath Ellen Parker, she had heard gunfire but, jerked out of the seat by Chernov's strong hand, she had felt relief that the woman was alive and doing something. She didn't know what it was until they got into the car but it didn't matter. Chernov was in charge and, in the moment of the sounds of guns, that was what she needed.

But now…

Now they were stopped in the rapidly spreading night and Chernov did not seem to know what to do. That terrified her more than anything had since the guns had torn into her trailer barely twelve hours earlier.

Suddenly Chernov was back in the car, her hands back on the steering wheel, but they were not moving.

"I don't know what the fuck I'm doing," Chernov said. Sharon did not think the woman was speaking to her.

"I never thought…" Chernov slowly shook her head. "Man, he was there just all of a sudden. All I wanted to do was leave." Her right hand released the wheel and slowly descended, touching the butt of the pistol she had shoved inside her jeans as if confirming reality. Snug against her right side, her body felt it for the first time, as if it had deliberately ignored the .45's heavy presence. At her waist, it was high compared to how she had worn the Berretta when she was back in the sandbox. She pulled her mind back from down range.

"I saw his gun," she said. Chernov smiled without humor touching her eyes. "I guess you never forget what you need to know." Finally, she turned and looked at Sharon. "Are you OK?"

Sharon nodded, afraid to speak.

"I am fucked up," Chernov said calmly. "And I don't know what to do, who to talk to, where to go." She smiled and again it did not touch her eyes.

"Talk to someone," Sharon said.

"Like who, little girl?" Chernov shook her head. "My old buddy from the police seems to have turned sour on us. I was in such a hurry to get you out of there that I didn't even stop to check on Parker." She stared back out the windshield. "I am fucked up," she said.

"Call a friend," Sharon said, her hands partially covering her mouth.

"Last time I did that, people tried to kill us."

"You have other friends," Sharon said. "Everyone has friends. I got friends in school."

Chernov remained silent, her eyes on the darkness. Finally, she took a slow breath.

"Well," she said, "I suppose it's time to find out if that's true."

Chapter 13

They let JJ into recovery for a moment. If it hadn't been for the tubes and wires, he might have been able to tell himself she was just sleeping. Then an RN guided him out into the hall.

"You can wait down the hall," she said. "At the intersection there's a small room. The surgeon will be there as soon as he changes and he can give you the latest news."

JJ allowed her to steer him to the room. The room was brightly painted, well lit, and had some magazines on a table. On the wall a flat screen television, its sound off, showed a newscaster silently mouthing words. He sat down and then stood up as Taylor came in.

"I don't know how long this is going to be," he said. "Why don't you go home?"

"I'm not crazy about leaving you here alone," she said.

"Doubt that I'm going to be alone very long," JJ said. "Lots of cops seem to be showing up."

"Not exactly my first choice for companionship," she said. "All right. I'll take your car home. Give me a yell as soon as you hear anything. I'll come and get you."

JJ nodded and handed her his car keys.

"Thanks," he said.

"Hell of a day," Taylor said as she left.

Though he had expected a parade of police, turf ownership already had been settled and only a pair of FBI agents spoke with him, though a tall black man stood behind them as they introduced themselves. The black man was a state trooper named Ross.

They asked the expected questions and JJ answered them as truthfully as he could. Yes, they were separated. It was because of his drinking. Yes, he was hoping for a reconciliation. He had been sober for four months and change. No, he did not know Karen was working on the task force. Yes, he had met her in Ohio eleven years previously when he had been detailed as the county sheriff's representative on yet another task force.

That he had been a deputy seemed to surprise one agent but not the other – someone had a more complete file.

Yes, she had been involved in a fatal shooting in Ohio. Another agent and a deputy were with her when they were ambushed. The agent was a friend of his and died at the scene. The deputy, also a friend, recovered from a massive facial wound.

JJ remembered the Ohio sunshine and following a blood trail into silent, green corn, a Remington pump shotgun pressed against his shoulder, and then peering into the face of one of the men that had tried to kill her. As his finger tightened on the trigger, a state trooper just said, "Deputy?" He had to say it twice but JJ had eased his grip.

"We have counselors," the first FBI agent said. "One of them will be checking in with her." He took a breath. "So far, it all looks righteous." He half smiled. "I'm not supposed to say anything, but cop to cop."

"Got it, thanks."

"We're going to have someone waiting here to meet with the doctor, get the prognosis, all that kind of thing, but he'll try to stay out of your way."

"Understood."

"Of course," the agent said. He looked to one side. "You want to hold on here until we get someone in place?"

"All right."

The FBI agent and the tall black man left, already listening to their cell phones.

JJ and the agent sat down. After a moment, JJ looked at the other man.

"Agent Barrows, is it?"

"Dave," Barrows said.

"I'm not real sure who's on first," JJ said. "Did I understand correctly that Karen works for you?"

"Yes, on the task force. She's heading up our profilers."

"And this had nothing to do with what you folks are investigating?"

"No," Barrows said, shaking his head. "She was helping the locals and everything went sideways."

"I asked her," Ellen Parker said from the door. She did not enter. "I knew both of them and when Beth called looking for someone she could trust, Karen came to mind."

85

JJ stood up and motioned to a chair.

"She's one to trust," JJ said as Ellen Parker sat down. "What did you see?"

"Beth saw it, or him, first," Parker said. "He had come in and then he pulled a gun. As I saw her draw her pistol, I grabbed Sharon, she's the little girl, and tried to hit the floor. I saw the man with the gun go down. Shots were fired outside. That was Karen. She came inside and I saw she was hurt. We called for help and waited for the ambulances."

"Ohio," JJ said. "Butler County. You were Thomas Luther Parker's granddaughter."

"Yes, sir," Ellen said.

"I'm thinking you didn't just wait for the ambulance," JJ said. "The other FBI agent I talked to mentioned you got someone to keep the towels in place."

"That's true," she said.

"You went outside," JJ said. "You wanted to make sure there wasn't another threat out there. You took Karen's gun with you."

"Yes, sir," she said. Her eyes were steady but Barrows' moved rapidly between the two.

"They haven't asked you about the shooting from ten years ago?"

"We know of it," Barrows said, nodding. "No need."

"Your task force," JJ said to Barrows, "if it has reviewed serial killer files from ten years ago, is working on another one."

"I cannot confirm nor deny," Barrows said, "but nice."

"Karen works as a profiler of those people. Easy guess."

JJ turned back to Ellen and looked at her.

"You went out of the restaurant," he said, "to try to stop any other bad guys who might have tried to go in. By yourself." He paused, letting the words hang for a moment. "You are pretty brave."

"So scared I wanted to pee myself," Ellen said.

"Your grandpa would have been proud," JJ said. Ellen's eyes went wide. "Thanks." JJ smiled. "That's quite a family you come from, Ms. Parker."

"Ellen, please," she said. She nodded. "Yes, they are pretty up and walking good."

Books finally got through to Tallman but didn't know how much he could or should say over the cell phone. Couldn't the government hear everything?

"Mister Tallman, it's Books."

"Good to hear from you." Tallman sounded like he had nothing more on his mind than tomorrow's weather.

"We've got a problem," Books said.

"One thing at a time," Tallman said. "I understand most of your business was concluded successfully."

"Yes, well, yes, you could say that," Books said, thinking of the methamphetamine in the back of the SUV. He wondered how many police were looking for the big vehicle now.

"Good, good. Now, I also understand there has been some additional difficulty."

"Yes, sir." Should he say they lost three people? Tallman seemed very calm, almost nonchalant.

"Very well, here's what we are going to do. Can you safely take down an address?"

"Yes, sir, just a moment." Books pulled over next to a farm stand closed for the night. He found a scrap of paper in his pocket but it took him a moment to find an old ballpoint pen. "Ready to go."

"I want you to go to Leonard's Garage, just a little south of Downingtown. I'll give you the street numbers in a second. I want you to park in the garage, not in the lot. It will be unlocked, the last bay from the road. Clear?"

"Yes, sir."

"Good. Later tonight, I'm not sure when, two people will come by. Don't leave the garage until both appear. One will pick up my property, the other probably will have some questions for you. When you leave, leave the vehicle there. Clear so far?"

"Absolutely, sir." Books licked his lips, remembering something Jacks had said but then tried to find a way of expressing himself without giving anything away. He gave up. "Sir, am I going to have to take off until this all blows over?"

"I don't think so, but we'll decide that later. Sometimes that happens, part of the job. We'll help you, of course, if it comes to that, but it may not be necessary."

"That's good news, Mr. Tallman."

"I am going to have one of our people call you."

"Yes, sir."

"Let me give you the street address of the garage."

Books copied the information down carefully, relieved that he finally had a sense of direction.

Thomas Tallman rubbed his lower lip. He did not want to make his next call, but the situation had significantly deteriorated. Deteriorated? If the television was to be believed two of his people were dead and one was wounded, "in serious condition." Only Books had walked away from the shootout. It would be best to handle this entirely in-house but time was critical. He had no option, if there was to be any chance at all, to outsource the task to recover the money.

The money, maybe as much as a hundred grand, that was the issue.

Keep the girl from talking? About what? People with guns. Tallman shrugged. One of his people survived the shootout. That was a major problem, one that, if he was still available, he would have Bobby Jacks deal with. He sighed.

But wasn't that the way of things? Just when you needed someone, they managed to make themselves unavailable.

Perhaps the best thing to do would be to just disappear for a while. Florida was nice in the spring. But, no, there were things that still had to be done. If the girl could be intercepted and the money recovered, fine. Might as well give it a try.

Outsourcing.

Tallman started to reach for his phone and then paused. Something…

All right, going after the trailer people was to recover his meth and his money and to send a message to the scattering of other drug producers who worked for him. Those particular people were easily sacrificed; once they got hooked by their own product, they became a liability in terms of both quality control and the criminal justice system. After all, speed freaks had trouble keeping their mouths shut.

The message was sent but was it enough? Tallman frowned, worried. For some time, he had thought he might have a leak in his organization. While such things happened on the periphery, compartmentalization kept problems away from the most important element in his organization.

Him.

Tallman suspected the leaker was higher. So did Jacks. But Bobby Jacks and most of his team were gone. Was it possible the leaker had tipped off the police and that was why Jacks was down?

That didn't make much sense. Perhaps there was something he was missing. What about Brunner, the police sergeant in Joyton? A very useful man, but what if he was playing both sides of the coin?

Tallman frowned again; he was getting nowhere except in making himself paranoid. All right, how to get something done without letting the leaker, if there was a leaker, know what was going on?

He picked up his cell phone from his desk. His mind made up, he did not hesitate to punch in the number.

"Good evening, Reverend," Tallman said.

"Thomas, good to hear your voice. How are things?"

Reverend Donaldson barely hid the contempt in his voice and Tallman felt anger but he shoved the reaction from his mind – getting the job done mattered, nothing else.

"I have a problem," he said. "I need to borrow one of your people."

"I think I understand, but you are not talking about needing someone for the transportation services we provide?" Tallman knew Donaldson was sitting on a shipment of methamphetamine to be delivered in the next few days to a distributer in Delaware County; good business relations required prompt delivery of expected goods and Tallman from time to time made use of Donaldson's willingness to provide that service.

"No."

"I see. I gather speed is of the essence."

"Exactly, Reverend. If it is going to be of any use, it has to happen quickly." Tallman paused. "It's primarily a recovery effort, but people are involved."

"Do you recall that fellow I mentioned when we last met?"

"He's the one I have in mind."

"I don't think there will be a problem with the people involved, but the fee…"

"I don't have a problem with the fee. The thing is, it has to be quickly done. We're in a bit of a race here. But I would prefer to play down any connection to my business."

"Ah, something subtle or, at least, something misdirected."

"That would be perfect."

"Well, because of the time issue, that may not be possible."

"I understand. I want as many of them taken down as possible, as many he can get to."

"Who are the people?"

"Two men, two women, and a kid. I'll provide him with a list of names along with some information."

"What is to be recovered?"

"Some money. We believe it was last in the possession of the little girl."

"I don't think I can guarantee that no one will associate his activities with yours but I'll ask him to see if there is something he can do to at least confuse the issue."

"I understand. I appreciate the effort."

"As for getting to the finish line first, not knowing the situation I cannot guarantee that can be done."

"For the recovery, ten percent of the money. For the rest, I'll pay you the fee you quoted plus twenty percent, twenty-five for the kid. I appreciate taking out the kid might be a bit more stressful than the usual," he said.

"That will certainly provide an incentive."

"Good. You need to get me his number. I have a person who can assist him."

"He really prefers to work alone."

"Two of his targets are in a hospital and there will be police. This person can get in and out with information he may need. He won't have to meet the person if he can be contacted by phone."

"Oh, I see. A reconnaissance; that makes sense. Very well, I will get you that number."

"Good. I also have a contact who can supply him with the information we have on the two primary targets, one of the women and a girl. He'll be the one with the list of names I mentioned. He'll need to meet the contact to pick up the paperwork."

"Excellent. When and where should he meet your contact?"

"This evening. The contact will be turning some things over to another of my employees early in the evening. I suggest coming by at ten. Leonard's Garage, Downingtown."

"The contact. A loose end?"

"He's on the list."

"Good. My man will appreciate that. Nothing like being thorough. Was there anything else?"

"No."

"Then have a good evening, Thomas. I will talk to you as soon as I have anything definitive for you."

90

The Reverend, James Donaldson stretched after putting his phone down. Leaning back in his chair, he knew he did not like talking with Tallman. The man, after all, was trash. An insult to the white race. But there was no denying he had his uses.

Donaldson was a handsome man, slightly shorter than average, his light brown hair carefully combed, giving no hint that it had been aided in overcoming his inherited male pattern baldness by the deft fingers of a surgeon.

Money could do anything short of miracles. After all, $45 to a mail order business had made him a minister.

His office was dimly lit, something he favored in order to more clearly see his computer's display. The knots in the pine paneling barely showed but the banner draped down behind his chair seemed to glow.

It was a confused amalgamation of starless Confederate crossed bars and a blue shield with a crown device over a sword splitting the reversed arms of a swastika. Donaldson believed that the elaborate emblem was representative of the problems the Aryan Nation faced. Since the sentencing of their leader slightly more than a year previously, the organization had continued in confused decline.

While a significant branch of the Aryan Nation had started from Klan roots in Pennsylvania's Potter County, things had gotten pretty damned muddled when their leader claimed to be forging an Aryan Nation-Muslim jihadist alliance four years after 9/11. Reverend Donaldson had argued that was trying for too much but had not been listened to.

Still, while chapters of the Aryan Nation around the country had folded during the past few years, his Church of Jesus Christ-Christian, located in a secluded compound in the woods of northern Chester County, had kept its head, and him, above water. Recruiting had had a small boost with the recession and Obama's election. Donaldson worked hard to keep links to other Christian Identity groups. Yes, the membership of the Aryan Nation, Nazis, Klan, and other groups tended to overlap significantly, but Donaldson thought it was just a question of time until all recognized the need for a single, unified white group to come together.

Preferably, with Donaldson in the hierarchy.

Until that golden day, the ongoing goal was to keep his church thriving and off the federal radar screen. And that was a challenge.

Inactive Aryan Nation groups tended to lose membership; giving Hitler salutes only took you so far. Someone had to do something, something the membership, even those not participating, could feel like they were a part of.

But the federal radar seemed to be ever present. They would use entrapment, RICO statutes, tax evasion, informers, whatever it took once they decided you had crossed the line from speech to action.

For Donaldson, the answer was sitting patiently in the last pew of his small chapel, watching as Donaldson emerged from the chapel office and walked down the aisle. He closed a book, carefully placing a marker within in, and then lay one of those electronic tablets on it. Well, whatever else he was, he was a reader. Donaldson saw the end of the bookmark sticking out; it was one of the ones his church distributed.

"Well," Donaldson said as he sat down, "thank you for coming over, John."

"You're welcome," John said. He had very ordinary glasses that, coupled with his slightly puffy features, made him appear like a middle-level office worker somewhere. He had a slight Southern accent that he worked to disguise but the effort did not hide the slightly mocking tone, though his eyes showed no humor.

"How are the bruises?"

"Pretty minor," John said. He made a show of moving his arm forward, slowly stretching it in front of him. "Still hurts to reach out, but she didn't crack any of my ribs. Just no fast moves." He brought his arm back. "I'm fine."

"We have a new situation," Donaldson said. "An opportunity."

"Oh?"

"A man I know needs some help." Donaldson shrugged. "He sells drugs. Is that a problem?"

"It's unclean, a sin," John said. His tone was indifferent, as if he knew how to recite the Aryan Nation catechism but didn't particularly care about it. Well, one made use of God's tools as best as one could.

"True," Donaldson said. "On the other hand, he has promised a sizeable reward if we are successful." He paused, feeling that he had to step carefully. "I know that you are looking for an opportunity to relocate. Unwanted attention."

John smiled and Donaldson wondered how much of the attention he had gained from killing the two lesbians truly was unwanted.

"Reverend," John said, his smile still present, "are you looking to move me on?"

"Of course not. You have been quite useful to the church. Striking at those two unclean abominations was good for our people and good for the church. But I recognize you have to make your own decisions. Remember, when you first arrived, you told me that you could not guarantee how long you would be available, and I appreciated your honesty."

"True." John nodded. "I don't think they've put things together, not yet. On the other hand, getting to Idaho will put me in a much more secure place."

"I agree," Donaldson said. "My conversations with some of our friends there were pretty positive."

"I could be useful to them, they said."

"Yes." Donaldson frowned a little. "So much of our movement started in Idaho but, to be honest, that seems to be where much of the chaos also has come from."

"I do like things to be orderly." John smiled.

"I think you are going to be very busy once you get there," Donaldson said.

"I'm looking forward to it. But to return to the current situation, what do they want to pay and for what?"

"Your part, if successful, will be 25 thousand, based on how many you can get to and a recovery he'd like performed. There are two men, two women, and a child, and he wants you to get to as many of them as you can. He also needs some money recovered. The money was last with the child. Now, two of the people on the list are in the hospital but he has a man who can get the lay of the land for you. I'll need your cell number."

"People from the shooting? Interesting. One's FBI." As he spoke, he brought out his cell phone from a pocket and turned it on.

"That's one of the women, I believe."

That had John's attention. He leaned forward, almost forgetting his open phone. He glanced at it and then showed Donaldson the display and the phone's number. Donaldson nodded and he put away the phone.

"And the other part is, if possible, it would be best if it looks like it has nothing to do with our drug dealer," Donaldson said as he wrote the number on a small sticky note.

"What do you mean?"

"An accident, perhaps. Or like the other two, a display of contempt. But not a simple shooting."

John smiled broadly, and there was nothing mocking in it.

"Not a problem," he said. "Lots of ways people can die in a hospital."

"You have a contact. A man you'll meet at Leonard's Garage in Downingtown. Just punch it into the GPS. The man will expect you at ten and will give you some specific information, including the list. He's going to see one of our dealer's people before that so, if you get there early, just wait."

"Understood. And the contact?"

"On the list. I gather he does not realize that."

"Good. I really don't like loose strings."

"Remember, he has the information you need to find the money, so don't get rash."

"Very well." John glanced at his watch. "I've got time to stop at McDonald's for dinner."

"You know that food isn't good for you," Donaldson said. "You need fiber, organic things free of contaminants. Pure food, pure body, pure race."

"I know, I know," John said. "Reverend, I appreciate you looking out for me, and you're right about the food, but temptation for me is a Double Quarter Pounder with Cheese." He shook his head and smiled. "I promise to eat some broccoli for lunch tomorrow."

"I am going to pray for you," Donaldson said.

"Thank you," John said. This time he sounded sincere.

Maybe it was a result of practice.

Chapter 14

Books knew the garage – he had conducted errands for Bobby Jacks from there – but, oddly enough, had not known its official name. As expected, the roll-up bay door at the far end was not locked. After parking the SUV inside, he went into the customer service office and got himself a soda. He was hungry but had no intention of leaving the garage.

The dim internal lights of the garage were on everywhere except in the back office, the one next to the rest rooms. Books went into it and made sure the door to the hall was firmly shut before turning on the lights. He looked around – it was an office, nothing more. File drawers, repair manuals, a computer on a desk that looked like it had made its way from some teacher's classroom, a chair that squeaked dangerously when he leaned back, and a door with two locks that exited out the back.

He fiddled with the computer but it required a password to go beyond the opening screen so he shut it down. Books looked around. This was where he had met Bobby Jacks and the others just that morning. He thought for a moment, remembering something he saw Jacks do.

Books walked to a set of tall file drawers. Crouching, he opened the bottom drawer.

Two boxes of 9mm ammunition lay along with a small automatic pistol. Books licked his lips; they probably belonged to Jacks and, judging by the hole that had blown out Bobby's back, he would not be back any time soon to claim his property.

Books took out the pistol, a compact Glock. He checked it and found it was loaded. He was careful not to touch the trigger – the Glock didn't have an external safety but used one located on its trigger. Even if he didn't keep it, it was probably worth more than five hundred bucks. He shrugged and slipped it into his jacket pocket.

He slid the drawer shut and, as he stood, heard a tapping at the front door. Looking around the office doorway, he saw a figure silhouetted by the outside lights. The man looked vaguely familiar but Books put his hand on the butt of his gun as he walked forward.

"Hey, Books," the man said. "You know me, I'm Chris." He wore a Coatesville Red Raider high school jacket but had a ratty face that looked like it had been half a century since he attended school. He was fidgeting, nervous about standing outside. "C'mon, man, let me in." Books, finally recognizing him, opened the door and he came in.

"You here for the stuff?" Books asked.

"Absolutely." Chris raised an athletic bag. "This be room enough? They weren't sure how much you found."

"Yeah, it's enough. Back here."

Books took the man to the SUV and raised the back hatch.

"Holy shit," the man said. "You've been driving around all day with this shit in the back? Holy shit." He shook his head as he started filling the bag.

Books said nothing. Finally, the man finished and carefully zipped the bag closed.

"All right, here's the deal," Chris said. His hands fluttered as he talked, a mannerism that seemed copied from somewhere, like someone trying to look cool. "Mr. Tallman has brought in some guy, a friend of a friend, to see if he can't get to the kid and get the money back. He wants you to cooperate with the man. Be careful what you say about our business, though."

"Sure, no problem."

Chris reached inside his jacket and Books' hand went to the pistol butt in the small of his back.

"Whoa, man," Chris said, showing both hands. "Nothing like that. I'm just a messenger, you know me, Chris, nothing heavy. They don't let me do anything heavy, you know?" His eyes were wild and he seemed unable to close his mouth. "I got some papers for that guy, all right?"

"All right," Books said.

"Just a messenger," he repeated. Chris slowly brought out a folded envelope and he passed it to Books.

"It's got info on the people Mr. Tallman wants dealt with. The rest is what he has on the woman who's with the kid. He said to say we got it from a cop."

"I know about that," Books said. "Jacks talked to him." He fingered the envelope; it was glued shut.

"Yeah," Chris said. "Jesus, what the hell happened out there?" He held up his hands. "Never mind, I don't want to know." He smiled weakly. "Anyway, if the guy wants you to help, Mr. Tallman says go ahead. If he doesn't, call him and we'll work on getting you out of sight for a while."

"He say where I was going to go?"

"Probably New Jersey," Chris said. He shrugged. "He said to say guys go over to Atlantic City when things get a little tight. I don't know about all that. But Mr. Tallman, he's got friends in Jersey; you sort of have to, I know that."

"All right."

"Meantime, you stay here and wait for the guy."

"All right."

Books walked Chris back to the door and let him out. He watched him get into his car and drive away. Books looked out the glass door for a while but there was nothing to see in the darkness.

New Jersey? Was that far enough away? There was something that didn't fit, something that caused him to frown as he tried to think. Something that Jacks said. He couldn't remember. He turned away from the door and walked back to the office.

Books dropped into the office chair. He felt like he hadn't slept in a week. And he needed something to eat. And what he'd like to do then…

Florida.

Jacks said if they needed to get out of sight they would go down to Florida. Florida. What the hell?

Friends in Jersey? It occurred to Books that a number of people deemed superfluous, a word and concept he remembered from his business magazine article, by organized crime got pink-slipped by being rolled into shallow graves in the Jersey Pine Barrens.

Before he could carry his thinking further, he heard a light tapping at the door. He craned his neck and saw a man through the glass. He used the back of his hand and again tapped.

Books walked up to the door but didn't open it.

The man looked very ordinary, glasses, maybe a little overweight, nondescript hair. Dark jeans, dark jacket, some kind of large book and a computer tablet in his hand at his side. He looked like no one at all. Books noticed he kept his other hand, fingers slightly spread, a little away from his side, as if signaling he meant no threat.

"Fuck it," Books said and twisted the lock handle.

"Hey," the man said. "OK if I come in?"

"Yeah, sure," Books said. He held the door, glancing around. A gray Toyota sat in the parking area but nothing else held his attention. The man entered and then waited while Books let the door close and locked it.

"They said you would have some papers for me," the man said.

"In the office," Books said.

The man smiled and made a kind of bow, waving his hand towards the rear. "After you," he said.

Books led the way and it was only after he had taken a few steps that he realized he had let the man get behind him. But nothing happened.

He picked up the envelope and handed it to the man.

"Thanks," he said. There was something about his tone that Books didn't like. He seemed to be treating everything, maybe Books, as some kind of joke that only he got.

"I'll get the light," Books said and closed the office door. This put him behind the man. He switched on the light. The man nodded his thanks and put his book and tablet down. He carefully cut open the envelope using a large pocket knife with a slightly curved blade. He rubbed his chin as he read.

Books looked at the book's cover; it was some kind of graphic novel, a comic book for adults. Dramatic fonts, people with swords, blood flying. Romans, maybe. The top of a book marker showed he was about a third of the way through.

"This is good information, detailed," he said as he reached the fourth page but he said nothing else until he was done. Then he looked at Books, still standing patiently.

"The thing I was told," the man said, "was that your boss wanted something recovered."

"Yeah, a blue backpack. It's got Mr. Tallman's money and he wants it back."

"And this woman and the kid have it."

"Yeah," Books said. "I don't know if you have any real chance. The two of them had met up with two other people, one of who was a cop of some kind."

"FBI Special Agent," the man said. "You made the news. She's been shot."

"Shit." Books had a sensation of walls moving towards him.

"She didn't die," the man said. "One of yours lived." Again, he seemed amused. "He's offering a bonus for the kid." He waited for a moment, until Books realized he was looking for confirmation.

"Yeah. She's picked up a guardian."

"So I read." The man seemed pleased. "He says you had been advised she was professionally trained."

"Trained?"

"She had been in the Army," he explained.

"Yeah, well, lots of people have been in the Army," Books said. "No big deal."

"Perhaps not," the man said. He paused. "There's a piece of this that doesn't make a lot of sense. Maybe you can help me."

"Maybe."

Books' response seemed to amuse the man, though his eyes gave nothing away and seemed to look through Books.

"Maybe. All right, your little team went to take down some people and the girl might have been a witness. Can't have any witnesses." There was the amused tone again.

"Yeah."

"Because they might identify one of you."

"Right."

"Well, one of you is alive and in police hands, according to the news people." The man said nothing for a moment, contenting himself to raising his eyebrows. "Probably not have much difficulty tying him to the people you all took down. It sounds like you four left lots and lots of bullets there and they are saying that FBI agent scooped a bunch of guns up even after she was shot." He shook his head and smiled. "You've got to love a woman of action. Anyway, then it becomes really fun. See, when they check on him, one of the things they will look for are 'known associates.' In fact, they will do that with the other two, the dead ones. I'm not a policeman and maybe it's too many hours spent watching TV, but doesn't that kind of mean they are going to know who you all are?"

Books didn't say anything but shook his head.

"Cat's out of the bag," the man said. "There are going to be a lot of fingers pointing at you all. Or is there something I'm missing?"

"I don't know," Books said. "They haven't told me anything."

"They haven't told you anything," the man said. He smiled. "That's not good news. For you, I think."

Remembering New Jersey, Books frowned.

"What do you mean?" he asked, though he already was answering his question.

"Your boss wants his money back, he wants the witness erased, but these are small matters, things not really important, right? But he farms the job out." The man smiled as if he had just told a joke. "In the meantime, what he really needs to do is cut the lines that lead back to him. Sure, every cop in the tri-state area knew he was involved as soon as they identified your friends if they have any knowledge about his operation at all. But proof usable in court would come only with one of you getting on the stand, dramatically pointing at him, and saying, 'Your honor, that's the motherfucker who hired us to murder that poor child and her parents.'" The man leaned forward. "See, I don't care what happens to you but I think he intends to use his own people to erase you after I leave to take care of your friend in the hospital."

Books said nothing, not realizing the lie John had told him.

The man leaned back, cocked his head to one side, and smiled.

Books looked at him for a moment, trying to figure out what the man wanted. "Why are you telling me all this?"

"Well," the man said, "I'm getting paid to bring back the money and deal with the others. A lot of people are going to be looking for that girl. I'd prefer it that some of them went looking for you instead. Might improve my chance of getting her."

"What the fuck?"

"Hey, don't get excited. But the reality is, if you stay here, maybe your own people will show up and you'll disappear forever and ever. Or have I misjudged the situation?"

Again, Books said nothing. The man made him uncomfortable, though he could not say why. Making jokes, teasing, even when serious, there was something... Disconnected was the word Books found. The man's eyes weren't a part of his smiles. They weren't a part of anything.

"I didn't think I had," the man said. "If you stay alive, though, that might draw some heat away from the people I'm after. That assumes, of course, that you are in a position to do some running."

Books shook his head, his lips tight.

"Hell," he said. "Yeah, you're probably right about what Tallman is up to. I already figured something wasn't right."

"You do seem to have stepped into it," the man said. "You can take off, but I imagine everyone wearing a badge is trying to find your car." He leaned forward again, as if trying for confidentiality. "And, of course, some of those badge-wearers are not to be trusted."

"No shit."

"On the other hand, you can go with me. Help me find the money and the girl and half the money is yours. Use it to get out of here. When they come looking for you, they run in circles. The harder you are to find, the more of them will be assigned to the hunt. That works well for me. See, I don't want you caught. My deal is, work with me, back me up when I make my move, and half of what we find is yours."

Books felt a faint surge of hope.

"You're not giving Mr. Tallman his money back?"

"The expression that comes to my mind is, 'Fuck Mr. Tallman.'" His smile broadened. "Look, if it is logical for him to remove you, then it is logical for him to remove me. I would rather not be removed as I have places to go, miles before I sleep, you see?"

Books nodded.

"Now, is it a problem for you that he wants me to take out one of the men you worked with?"

"Who is it?"

"A man named Jones."

Remembering Jonesy, Books shook his head.

"No, fuck him. He almost shot me."

"All right," the man said. "Yeah, we'll knock down some of the people he wants gone if we can, just so he doesn't realize what we're up to. But we keep the money and we split it and we use it to travel somewhere we'd be a bit more welcome than eastern Pennsylvania." He shook his head. "Not really my kind of place anyway."

"I don't think you've got much of a chance," Books said. "They're probably walking into a TV station or something right now. I think we blew it."

"Maybe not," the man said and smiled. "I think I know who she's going to run to. All we have to do is stir things up, get her to start running again, and then sit on where she wants to be and we're safe at first."

"Where do you think she'll go and how do you know she isn't already there?"

"Woman who wrote a story about her," the man said and then he smiled again. "Another woman. If she was with her, it would be all over the news. Reporters love reporting about themselves more than anything else."

"The woman she went to meet at the pizza place?" Books grinned. "That would be crazy."

"Women go to those they trust," the man said seriously. "She knows that woman, her name is Parker. She's under stress, she'll go to the people she trusts."

"You know the agent is in the hospital."

"Along with your guy."

"He's not my guy," Books said. "What I wanted to say is, I may be able to help with the hospital."

"Oh? We have a guy scouting it for us."

"Has he worked there?"

"Probably not."

"I did."

"And the stars are in alignment," the man said. "Lovely, just lovely. What did you do there?"

"I was a paramedic, covered some nursing homes. We were in and out of Brandywine all the time."

"We need a way to get in that won't get us noticed."

"There are a couple of ways to do that."

"Lovely," the man said. "Glad to have you as a partner."

"All right," Books said. "I'm Books. What do they call you?"

The man's smile broadened.

"Do you listen to any blues?"

"Music? Sure, a little."

"Call me Doctor John," the man said. His fingers danced in the air in front of him. "I play a killer piano."

"Whatever, Doc."

The man chuckled and led the way out of the garage. Books had never heard of The Night Tripper, not yet.

"Where are we going to go?" Sharon asked.

"You're right," Chernov said as they drove through the darkness. "Everyone has someone they can talk to. "She grimaced. "Thing that happens is, you get so narrow in your field of view you stop seeing options. So, what we do is, we get back to Ellen Parker. First thing, though, is we need a different car. Too many people have seen this one."

"Are you going to steal one?"

"No," Chernov said. "I have another friend and she may have a spare."

"Can your friend let us stay with her?"

"She would if I asked, but I'm not going to ask."

"Why not?"

"I don't want to drag anyone else in on this," Chernov said. "You know?"

"I guess."

"She lives near here. Not far."

"I have to pee."

"We'll take care of that when we get to her home."

"All right," Sharon said.

It took twenty minutes before Chernov found the apartment building she wanted. She circled around it and parked in back. She backed into a slot to one side of a blue trash dumpster and then shut off the engine.

"I hope she's home," she said.

"Why don't you call her?"

"Low on juice," she said. She took a minute and fished out the spare .45 round from the glove compartment. Then she ejected the clip, fed the round into it, and slid the clip back into the pistol.

"Why did you do that?" Sharon asked.

"You never know," Chernov said. She squinted into the darkness, looking at the apartments. "Let's go see if she's home."

"OK." Sharon reached for her backpack.

They used the parking lot entrance and Chernov led the way to the stairs. They went up one flight and stopped in front of a door labeled "2F." Chernov forced a smile at Sharon and then knocked softly on the door.

The eyehole in the door dimmed and then brightened. The door opened and a tall blond woman, wearing jeans and a Notre Dame sweatshirt, stood before them, shaking her head, trying to look severe but failing as a smile crept in.

"Talk about bad pennies," she said in a husky voice. Burn scars ran up the left side of her throat, stopping at her earlobe.

"Hey, jarhead," Chernov said and the two women embraced. Finally, they separated. "This is Sharon."

"Everyone calls me Sherrie," the girl corrected.

"I'm Hannah, Sherrie," the tall woman said. "Come on in and sit a spell."

103

They followed her into a small living room. A flat screen television was on but the sound was muted.

"BBC," Hannah said, waving at the screen. "Can't stand CNN. Like watching a game show."

"Try Fox," Chernov said, dropping into a chair.

"Barf," Hannah said. "Anyone have to go to the bathroom?"

"We've been on the road, sure."

"That's what I hear," Hannah said. "Down the hall, straight ahead. Little girls go first."

"Good," Sharon said and hurried down the hall.

"It's been on the local news," Hannah said to Chernov. "Sherrie's people taken out and then some kind of gun fight at a pizza place. You were identified by name and they had a particularly terrible picture of you. I think it was your driver's license. So was Ellen Parker. They had a better picture of her."

"'Some kind' is right." Chernov bit her lower lip.

"Are you OK?"

"They never touched me."

"Not what I meant, but it's a start. You guys hungry?"

"Not me, but maybe her."

"I'll get something running," Hannah said, getting up. "Follow me to my lair."

Chernov went with her into the small kitchen. Hannah opened the refrigerator. They heard a toilet flush.

"Sherrie," Hannah called as she examined food containers, "you up for food?"

"I'm hungry," she said.

"What sounds good? I have some stew…"

"Can I have a grilled cheese? My Mom makes me grilled cheese," Sharon said as she stood in the kitchen doorway. Then the little girl swayed as the tears came.

Chernov swept her up and Hannah saw the girl's arms cling tightly to her. Chernov sat down, closed her eyes and shook her head.

"Today has really sucked," she said as Sharon cried into her neck.

"I didn't think it'd been a good one," Hannah said. She waited a moment and then began slicing cheese.

After some time, five minutes on the kitchen clock, an age on Sharon's calendar, the crying slowly stopped. Sharon used a tissue to wipe her eyes and blow her nose and Hannah saw, even after Chernov put her down, the young girl stayed close.

"I'm OK," Sharon said. "I just miss her."

"I know," Chernov said. "Losing someone you love is hard."

Sharon nodded.

"Mommy said that people we love stay with us forever."

"She might be right. I'm still trying to figure that out."

"I think she is," Sharon said. She looked up at Sharon and Hannah saw a steadiness in her eyes that was surprising. "Keep thinking about it."

Chernov grinned crookedly in reply and looked at Hannah, shaking her head.

"Food," Hannah said, and Sharon nodded.

Hannah made grilled cheese for Sharon and, though she shook her head no, one for Chernov. After the girl ate, she took off her shoes and curled up on the living room couch while Chernov and Hannah returned to the kitchen.

"So," Hannah said. "You stay here and we call for the cavalry. We set up a perimeter until they arrive. Problem solved."

"No," Chernov said. "They've followed us everywhere we've gone. I think the bad guys have their hooks into some cops, at least one. That's why they almost caught us before the firefight. Hell, that's why the firefight, I think."

"I have an Ithaca pump under my bed, girl, and so many handguns I've lost count. They won't make it to the perimeter wire."

"Well, Hoo-fucking-ah."

"That's, 'Uh-rah,' doggie. Try and say it the Marine way." Hannah grinned. "Really, it's not a problem. And running around the state, someone's going to notice you."

"No running. Fuck running." Chernov suddenly was serious. "I'm going to make one call. Arrange a meeting where I can see what's coming. There's this reporter…"

"Ellen?" Hannah asked. "I said she was on the news. Doesn't seem to have aged much since she did that article about us. I've been following her online. Sure, she's a straight arrow. But, shit, she almost got taken out when they tried for you in the pizza place. You don't need a representative of the press; you need a platoon of Marines."

"Got one handy?"

"Hell, Quantico's a long way to drive. So what's your plan?"

"I call Ellen. I tell her to bring her Fee-Bee friend and…"

"She can't," Hannah said. "Her friend, that's Karen Deevers, right? Took a round after dropping two baddies outside your pizza place."

"No, fuck no." Chernov's eyes went wide.

"She's alive." Hannah got up and walked over to a small table and took a laptop off of it. She flipped the lid up and, after a second, typed a few keys. "Here you go," she said, handing the machine to Chernov.

Chernov saw a local news website and quickly read about herself and Sharon. As she read, her lips tightened. Finally, she leaned back.

"Shit."

"No shit," Hannah agreed. "So, tell me again your plan."

"All right," Chernov said. "I call Ellen. I ask her to meet us somewhere, some place that no one can sneak up on us."

"And she brings the cavalry with her, not just one lone Special Agent."

"Yeah, all right."

"You know," Hannah said, "you could have her come here."

"No," Chernov said. "Nice apartment, but only one way in and one way out. I have to assume that the bad guys are tapped into the police. They'll be burning rubber to get to us before her and if it happens they are closer…"

"This place would look like Fallujah," Hannah said. She shrugged. "Well, the rents are a little too high anyway."

"No, seriously. If anything goes sour, I don't want anyone here hurt."

"Roger that." Hannah thought. "All right, here's what we do. I take you to your rendezvous. I watch your back until Ellen and her cavalry arrive. Then I go home and wait for Ellen to get nominated for another Pulitzer. Maybe this time she makes it."

"Sounds like a plan, except for the part of you coming along."

"I don't like it, Beth," Hannah said. "Not you going alone. We don't know how many turds are going to show up, if any. Are you getting into some kind of last stand mentality?"

"Hey, we're not in group therapy anymore."

"You're not," Hannah said. "I still go."

"Is it helping?"

"Yeah," Hannah said. "I got most of the big pieces done with the doc, he was great with that eye movement stuff, but the support is nice and I get to be the big sister to the youngsters. Gives me a sense of self importance."

"Well, yeah, Marine and all – you need some ego help."

"I'm going to go with you, lady."

"I just need your car."

"Fuck you, I'm going to go with you."

Chernov said nothing for a moment.

"Why?" she asked.

"You already know," Hannah said. "We don't, not ever, leave any of our own behind." She was serious, the kidding in her voice gone, and her eyes were steady.

"I hear that," Chernov said, her voice small. "Thanks, jarhead."

"Not a problem, doggie," Hannah said and nodded. "Hell, maybe Ellen will write a book this time. Get made into a movie; she'll be played by Bruce Willis." This was a small game the two women had played before.

"And you by Scarlett Johanssen."

"My hair's too short, her butt's too small, and she doesn't have my charming scars."

"Makeup will take care of all that."

"Yeah? Well, Helen Hunt would play you."

"Really? She's got great eyes."

"We'd have to cut her hair, of course, maybe with a gas-powered grass trimmer. Then it'll match your mop."

"Why is it I can't get any respect?"

"Go use the bathroom," Hannah said. "Maybe you will if you take a shower. Clean towels are the blue ones."

"Thanks." Chernov stood and looked over at Sharon, who was asleep, her blue backpack on the floor. She looked back at Hannah. "I'm carrying. A .45 auto."

"I guess you know how to use it."

"Apparently. But it's been so long since I was shown it, all my time was with the Berretta 9mm. Can you give me a hand cleaning it?"

"Let me have it," Hannah said, holding out her hand. She freed the clip and pulled the slide to the rear, flipping a round onto the table. She checked that the chamber was clear and locked the slide back.

"A very manly handgun, young lady," Hannah said, examining it. "You going all butch on me?"

"I think it belonged to Sharon's people," Chernov said. "I found it in the backpack."

"It's a good one," Hannah said. "Springfield Armory does nice work. Go take your shower and I'll break it down."

"Thanks."

Chernov let the hot water beat on her and borrowed some of Hannah's shampoo. By the time she emerged from the bathroom she felt something like human again. She was still rubbing a towel into her hair when she walked into the kitchen.

On the table were a half dozen handguns, most dark gray or black, a short pump shotgun, and a black, semi-automatic rifle.

"Jeez Louise," Chernov said. "You got yourself an M-4?"

"No, it was a gift. Not automatic. It's in .223. Nice for plinking. Now, I cleaned up your pistol."

"Thanks."

"No problem. I was thinking maybe you would prefer something with a little less kick. But I don't have a Berretta. The only nine I have is this old Glock. It's very nice, a good shooter, but the safety is in the trigger so you have to be careful."

"I'll keep the .45."

"Well, thought you would, since you know the damned thing works. Here's another .45, 1911 style, from Kimber. Here's a pair of .40s, this is actually a .10mm, and this little snubby is just a .38. Belonged to my Dad, back when he flew in 'Nam. Still works but you have to be pretty close for anything like accuracy. Anyway, if you want a second gun, something for backup, take one."

"The idea is to avoid a firefight." She picked up the .38 and checked the cylinder was empty.

"I hope that's a shared idea," Hannah said. "When are you going to call Ellen?"

"Tomorrow morning."

"Long drive for her, all the way from Philly."

"I don't think she'll be there. I figure she'll be a lot closer."

"Brandywine? Sure, she'll wait to talk to the Feeb." Hannah smiled. "I remember how solicitous she was when she did that article on us. Some kind of mother hen. So, yeah, she'll be hanging close until she finds out about the agent."

"Maybe things will have settled down by then."

"Do they ever?"

Chapter 15

Sergeant Don Brunner wanted to step into a corner somewhere and throw up. The call from Tallman had not been expected and, of all the things that Tallman might have wanted, walking the halls of Brandywine Hospital looking for people was not anything Brunner would have recommended.

After his last conversation with Jacks – Brunner wondered if it was the last phone conversation Jacks had with anyone – he had tried to figure out how he could hide the trail that connected him to Elizabeth Chernov and that damned brat. People knew he had talked to her on the department main line. No hiding that. Of course, his calls to Jacks and Tallman had been on his throw-away cell. That blurred but did not erase the trail.

Tallman's command to reconnoiter the hospital seemed like stretching things entirely too far but the exchange might be worth it. Find out where Jonesy and the Fed were, pass the info onto Tallman's substitute hitter, and the hitter would go on to take out Chernov and the kid. That would erase the trail.

Sure, Chernov had been in the department with him and he liked her. But he liked the money from Tallman more and staying out of jail he liked even more than that. So, quid pro quo or whatever the hell the saying was.

The hospital's halls were laid out by someone who liked to run people through mazes. Parallel hallways formed ladder-like designs that occasionally seemed to dead-end and just as occasionally linked up to another crossing hall and sometimes a whole other building.

But finding what he wanted was not that hard. The wounded perpetrator's location in the surgical recovery suite was marked by a small cluster of people who could only be cops whether in uniform or plain clothes. He nodded to people as if he was supposed to be there but kept moving. As he watched, a pair of officers peeled off the small group and headed out, leaving only two county deputies. Of the two, one was a man who looked like he liked to work out with weights, while the other was older. The older one was listening to a cell phone and Brunner got the impression they were about to be sent home for the night.

No security left? That didn't seem likely but at least there were only two.

Finding the FBI agent was a little more difficult only because he didn't want to ask directions. He checked the other areas of recovery and intensive care but she wasn't there. It wasn't until he realized that she was in a regular room on another floor that his search was successful.

As he turned off the elevator, again there was a small cluster of police, all in plain clothes. As he approached, he glanced to his left. Two people were in the waiting area, a thin woman who looked up as he passed and a strong-looking man idly leafing through a magazine. Then nearly all the people in the hall turned and walked towards him.

Fear raced through Brunner but the FBI agents barely nodded on their way to the elevators. Only two remained in the hall. He assumed both were FBI, with one a tall, older black man with white in his hair and the other looking like he had spent his college years playing football.

Brunner turned around, walking back the way he came. Neither man in front of the agent's room noticed him. Past the waiting area he found a restroom. He went in and checked the stalls. Alone, he pulled out his phone and, reading from a page in his notepad, he punched in a number.

"Yes?" Whoever it was, the voice wasn't familiar to Brunner.

"Found them," he said. "Do you know the hospital?"

"Hold on, let me check." There was a pause that quickly passed.

"Probably. Tell me where they are and, if I need directions, I'll say so."

"All right," Brunner said. "Your man is still in recovery. I didn't ask questions but it looks like they're going to have an over-watch on him, plus you have the medical people. But there aren't many."

"OK, just a second." A moment later, the speaker returned. "East side or west side?"

"East."

"OK, we got it. Where's the other?"

"In a regular room. I think she's solo in there but it was hard to see inside. Most of the cops have left but there are still two outside her door. Down the hall are a couple of people, her husband, I think, and some other woman in the waiting room."

"Room number?"

Brunner gave it and again waited while the speaker checked in with something or someone.

"OK, we know where that is. The woman you saw in the waiting room, a cop?"

"No, no. I think she's a reporter."

"Describe her."

Brunner described Ellen Parker and he heard a chuckle when he finished.

"'Raw-boned,' indeed. All right. What you want to do now is get out of Dodge."

Brunner didn't try to come up with a witty reply. He slipped his phone into his pocket and, as quickly as he dared, walked down the hall to the elevator.

A few minutes later, he was walking to his car. The official-looking cars bunched around the entrance to the ER had thinned out, though whether because they were gone or because they had moved out of the way was not clear.

He pulled into the long drive from the parking area and drove towards the exit, feeling like he could breathe again.

He was less than fifty yards from the exit when he saw the first of a half dozen police cars, marked and unmarked, violently turning onto the drive. All had in common their lights were flashing and they were not using their sirens.

"Shit." He edged to the shoulder and stopped as the cars raced past him, obviously intent on something very serious.

It occurred to Brunner that he could call Tallman's hitter. It also occurred to him that he'd done enough for one day. He took out his phone and turned it off. As the last police car whipped past, he eased back out onto the drive and carefully drove up to the exit.

Though the light was in his favor, Brunner carefully looked in both directions. Cops intent on getting some place in a hurry could develop tunnel vision just like anyone else and he didn't want a Ford Taurus Police Interceptor intercepting him through the driver's door. It was clear and he pulled out, smiling – an Interceptor intercepting seemed to be the funniest thing he had heard all day.

JJ had gotten up to get a can of soda for himself and Ellen Parker when he heard the phones of the two men in front of Karen's room go off at the same time. The noise was just enough to attract his attention and he looked towards them with little interest; the agents and other police had their phones chiming, beeping, buzzing, and serenading pretty much all evening.

The gun that appeared in Ross's hand suggested this was not routine business. Both men, even as they listened to their phones, were looking up and down the hall. The FBI agent, the one named Barrows, motioned JJ back towards the waiting area. He complied, though it was a struggle not to run down the hall.

"What's going on?" Ellen asked, sitting up.

"I don't know," JJ said, "but I think they just went on alert for a threat."

"A threat to Karen?" Ellen's eyes were wide. JJ held up a hand.

"We wait here, out of the way." He looked up and down the hall. "I don't see…"

Footsteps pounded down the hall and a pair of FBI agents, their identification held up in front of them, though JJ believed both had been in front of Karen's room within the past fifteen minutes, ran down the hall. Both men looked at and then ignored JJ and Ellen.

Over the next fifteen minutes, more police officers arrived. Some were dispatched to other areas of the hospital, probably to provide perimeter security, JJ thought. But Ross and Barrows never left Karen's door.

JJ waited until things appeared to be stabilized. Ross had put away his gun but an agent stood near the waiting area watching the nurses' station and elevators with a black shotgun in his hands and yellow FBI on the back of his blue windbreaker. He walked down the hall to her door.

"Sir?" the agent with the shotgun asked but Barrows gave him a thumbs up and he turned back to the elevators.

"What's going on?"

"We got a tip," Barrows said. He nodded at Ross. "It came through the staties. Phil, whatever you can."

"Confidential informant called it in," Ross said. "He said the people Karen faced, the ones trying for the kid, have sent in someone to try to take her out."

"Why? Drug people don't like to mess with cops, especially feds."

"We don't know why and you're right, that's usually the case. In the meantime, we are trying to get the hospital locked down. Big place, lots of ways in and out, so we started with her front door and are pushing the perimeter outward. Elevators, stairwells, entrances."

"All right, got it. How reliable is the CI?"

"Supposedly, very." Ross shrugged. "You never really know."

"I understand. Can I look in on Karen?"

Ross glanced at Barrows.

"Sure. Remember what the doc said."

"I know, I know, don't wake her up." He stepped between the two and entered Karen's room.

She still slept, unaware of the drama taking place outside her room. JJ stared at her face, dimly lit by a small lamp. Even with wires, tubes and a hanging bag of fluid, she still was the most beautiful woman he had ever loved. He had a moment when he wondered how he had allowed himself to screw things up so badly.

JJ walked back to the door and put his head out.

"Guys," he said, "I'm going to sit in here for a while. She's asleep."

It was Barrows' turn to shrug.

"All right. We'll let you know if anything happens."

JJ took a seat in the shadows. His eyes remained on Karen, even when he reached inside his jacket and pulled out a large automatic handgun. In his hands it seemed small. He checked the safety was on and returned it to its holster at his waist. Then he leaned forward, elbows on knees, and waited.

Books led the way into the hospital. Getting past the hospital security was not a thing he wanted to chance; instead, he took Doctor John to a door that was propped open by a broken brick.

"Smokers use this," he whispered and John grinned.

Books, pleased that his first choice for entry had worked, moved cautiously into what appeared to be a storage area. Before exiting to a hall, he carefully cracked open the door, listened for a moment, and then stepped out.

"We can use the stairs," he said and John nodded.

With the halls deserted, getting to the recovery area was easy.

"Probably be some medical staff at the central location," Books said. He kept his voice barely above a whisper. "And your guy said cops."

"We'll just see if it's possible. No sense being crazy."

Books wasn't sure if John's comment was reassuring. As they walked down the hall, they watched as, up ahead, a uniformed policeman walked across the hall and disappeared to their left. Books tried to stop but John gently shoved him.

They turned into the double doors the policeman had come through, entered a short hall with a monitoring station. A woman wearing pale blue scrubs, an iPad glowing on her desk, looked up, surprised.

"Can I help you, gentlemen?"

"I'm Doctor John." He stepped towards her and turned his head slightly. "Find him."

Books walked past the station and turned to his right. His heart pounded hard enough he could hear it. What was John doing with the nurse?

Jonesy lay in a reclined bed with several electronic devices displaying medical gibberish around him. Wires led away from him and wove into a single strand that disappeared over his shoulder.

He looked totally fucked up, Books decided.

"This our boy?" John asked, silent in his approach.

Books nodded and John stepped up to the head of the bed. He looked at the displays.

"He's not doing very well," he said, and then Books saw the knife. John lifted the thin blanket covering Jonesy, folded it over, and jabbed the knife through it.

"Spray," he explained. Then he stabbed Jonesy in the throat. The blanket caught the blood but quickly became sodden as John sawed it up and down. He pulled the knife free, glanced at the displays, and the knife disappeared.

He was smiling. Books suddenly realized he had been smiling the whole time.

"Time for contestant number two," he said.

Books felt frozen. This was too obvious. Wasn't there something they could have done to disguise the killing? And the expression on John's face as he worked had been like that of someone doing something that required all of his attention and something he enjoyed, like a guy watching porn. But his eyes had been blank, expressionless. Disconnected.

"Got to go back down the hall," Books said. He led the way out of the recovery room. He glanced at the monitoring station but saw nothing, which, in its own way, was as scary as watching John cut Jonesy's throat.

As they stepped into the hall, they heard the sound of a toilet flush.

"Keep going," John said. "He'll wash his hands."

Whether or not the policeman practiced personal hygiene remained unknown. It was enough for Books that they made it undiscovered to the stairs. He started to go up when John grabbed his arm.

"Down," he whispered. "They're coming." He took the stairs two at a time. Books followed, nearly falling when he caught his heel. They got to the bottom and Books heard feet pounding their way up the stairs above them.

"Get us out of here," John whispered.

Books, his lips tight, led them out of the stairwell and followed the basement hall back to the storage room. They went into it, heading for the exit. Books barked his shin on something hidden in the dimly lit room but he did not slow down.

In a few strides, they were out of the hospital and in John's car. Books was glad that they had used one of the staff parking slots.

"Well," John said, "that was interesting." He looked around and pushed his glasses up on the bridge of his nose. "Move us over to the visitor's parking area."

"Shit, man," Books said. He bit his lip and shook his head as he started the car. "Where did they all come from?"

"Where, indeed?"

"No way are we going to get to that FBI woman." He followed the road around the hospital.

"I agree." John seemed unruffled. "But remember, those were just people on Tallman's list. We're really just interested in two, the two with the money."

"Yeah, right. So now what?" The visitor's parking area was quite large and he had expected it to be empty, this close to midnight. But it looked like a lot of the night staff used it rather than the employee's area closer to the main road.

"Ellen Parker is somewhere in that hospital. When she comes out, it will be to guide us to the money."

"If she comes out." He pulled in between two cars that gave a fairly unobstructed view of the entrance.

"Oh, I think she will. We've stirred the pot. She'll be worried. She'll call. She'll go."

"I hope you're right."

"I usually am."

Day Two

Chapter 16

Ellen Parker waited for JJ to return but he did not. She assumed he intended to wait in Karen's room until everything was secure, whenever that might be.

Her memory of JJ went back to Ohio, back when her grandfather still lived. Her family, she remembered, gathered on a hillside. JJ, wearing his deputy's uniform, walked up to them. John Wesley Parker, her uncle, and Thomas Luther Parker, her grandfather and the man she suspected of hunting down the men who killed her cousin, watched him from the time he got out of his car. The two had been talking, Korea, Vietnam, something. JJ introduced himself and shook her hand, firmly, not in the dainty way adults do with children. JJ said the business of the Steel Riders, the killers of her cousin, was over.

He had said it to her grandfather, looking him in the eye. Grandpa Tom thought for a moment and then said he thought it was. Before walking down the hill, JJ had handed something to Grandpa Tom, an old shotgun shell Tom said. It wasn't old, not at all, and Tom put it on the mantle in the living room. Ellen had always wondered what the shell meant but, even after her grandfather's death, John Wesley never said.

She kept moving in her chair; it was too comfortable and she didn't want to go to sleep. Finally, she stood, stretched, and paced in the small area.

As she turned at the end of what she thought of as a "lap," she saw one of the people in front of Karen's room walk towards her. That was when she realized there were now four officers, all plain clothes though two wore blue windbreakers with FBI in large yellow letters on the back.

"We met," the tall, black man with white in his hair said, "but we didn't speak. I'm Phillip Ross, State Police."

Ellen held out her hand and Ross was surprised at her firm grip.

"I remember seeing you," she said.

"We've got a serious situation," Ross said. He motioned towards the waiting area. "We received information that an attempt on Agent Deever's life might be made."

Ellen's eyes went wide, her drowsiness gone.

"It gets worse. Someone got to the perpetrator here in the hospital and killed him. And the nurse on duty at his station." Ross started to say something else but stopped himself. "They're going to do a full search, top to bottom."

"I understand."

"That friend of yours, the one guarding the kid. Chernov?"

"Beth Chernov," Ellen said.

"You need to get in touch with her and get her to come in."

"I'd do that but her phone isn't picking up. All I get is diverted to her voice mail."

"Shit." Ross ran his hand through his short hair and Ellen saw how tired he was. He looked up. "Something has come together," he said. "We're not sure how, but the case Karen was working on and the situation Chernov is in have come together."

"What do you mean?"

"Background only." He waited.

"Agreed."

"You heard JJ's analysis of Karen's assignment. The guy we're looking for, he's also involved in this thing with the little girl."

"How do you know that?" She shook her head. "He's working for some drug organization? A serial killer?"

"A big-time killer," Ross said. "We've been tracking him across four states." He paused and Ellen saw him weighing his next words and then finally deciding. "He's made use of a variety of groups for cover and movement. He started with some drug dealers, working for them, we think, as a hit man but did his thing on the side. He got passed along. We're not sure who he's with here in Pennsylvania but we suspect it's a white supremacist group, one close by."

"He killed the nurse and the bad guy?"

"Yes, definitely on the nurse, probably on the guy, who is David Allen Jones, by the way, if you missed the briefing."

"He has a signature," Ellen said. "That's why you know he killed the nurse."

"He does. We're not releasing it."

"I understand." Her brow furrowed slightly. "White supremacist groups nearby? There aren't that many, not here in Chester County. You haven't been able to pin down who's covering him?"

"We're working on it."

Ellen nodded. Ross's response could be cop-speak for anything from, "We have no idea" to "We're all over it but we're damned if we're to give it away to some reporter." A look in Ross's eyes led her to suspect it was the latter.

"I don't know where Beth is," she said.

"If you can think of anything, let us know." He grimaced, shaking his head. "He's looking for her and the little girl, we think. Probably because they think the kid has a bunch of money. This guy, he's a bad one. And not stupid. If he can figure something out, he'll use it."

Ellen judged from what Ross had said that he had information from somewhere – there was too much in what he had just said to be guesswork – and she guessed an informant within the drug organization was the source but she did not ask further about the information.

"What do you want me to do?"

"Just keep trying to get in touch with her," Ross said. He forced a smile. "It would be great if she just decided to drive up to one of our barracks somewhere. But in the meantime, we're getting wall to wall police here and…" He paused, looking at Ellen. "What?"

"Earlier," she said. "A while ago. Police officer. He wore a shoulder patch. New Joyton. Was he one of your reinforcements?"

"No," he said. "When was that?"

"When your group broke up," Ellen said. "I didn't notice the time."

"What got your attention?"

"He didn't talk to you," she said. "He started down the hall, your group broke up, went past him, and then he turned around and went back the way he came."

"He should not have been on this floor," Ross said. "Everyone up here was federal or state. The county had the ground floor. None of the local police were being used." His eyes narrowed.

"Excuse me," he said. "I want to make some calls." With that, Ross turned abruptly and walked back down the hall. He did not pull his cell phone out of his pocket until he was at Karen's room, too far for Ellen to hear anything.

Where was Beth and why didn't she answer her phone?

"What if she doesn't come out?" Books asked. It seemed to be a fair question. There were now seven police cars that he could identify, an unknown number that he could not, and Ellen Parker had yet to appear. He had thought Parker would appear right after the discovery of Jonesy's death, but that had been an hour ago. He glanced at his watch as John remained silently studying his tablet.

"I'm working on it," John finally said. "Just tell me if they start checking the cars around us." He smiled but didn't raise his eyes. "That would suggest we were in trouble."

Books thought he already was. Sure, there was the manhunt on to find him, and he assumed if Jonesy had a chance to rat him out, the asshole did it in a heartbeat.

Which took him to what he thought might be his greatest trouble. Doctor John's killing of Jonesy and, he presumed, the nurse was quick and silent, sure, but gave away what they were trying to do. Now the place was crawling with cops and, sooner or later, they would check every car in every one of the hospital lots.

That's what cops did. They checked things. They weren't Sherlock Holmes, none of them were brilliant that he knew of, but they checked every damned thing and if you made the smallest mistake, they had you.

But here they sat, waiting for some reporter named Parker to appear. Yeah, John said Chernov would contact her again and, like a good little reporter, she would go running. Sure, that was probably true. In the meantime, they were sitting ducks.

And no Parker.

John's masterful logic was maybe full of holes. Maybe it was what he wanted to believe. Books' lips were tight. There was the thing about the killings. John was into it, into killing. He wasn't like Jacks; this wasn't just business to him. He liked it.

This was not a good thing, Books thought. Maybe it was time to start thinking about making his own plans.

Then he saw Ellen Parker come out of the hospital.

Ellen tried Chernov's cell one more time and again was greeted by a transfer to her voice mail. She put her phone away and tried to think.

She had turned off her phone and had not called her; Ellen guessed Chernov blamed her for the arrival of the bad guys at the pizza shop. She couldn't see how it was her fault but maybe Chernov was running on "combat rules;" simply stated, those rules narrowed everything down into two categories, threat and not. Maybe she figured Ellen had screwed up in some way and was no longer a safe contact.

Who else did Chernov know? She had a brother somewhere. Maine? Vermont? Well, if she was running to him that was fine. The further away she and Sharon were the better.

But if she was still in the local area, where would she go?

Well, there was the man who owned the cabin she stayed in. Mr. Lowenstein had hired her for his furniture business but it soon became clear Chernov was not a "people person." Maybe it was his brother who had served in the Army in Vietnam, maybe it was his son who did a tour with the Air Force in Afghanistan, but he had kind of adopted the angry young woman and gave her a place to stay even after he fired her from the store.

All right, one possibility. Who else?

The article, the one including Chernov, had been about women coming back from the war. Beth had been one of a small group going to the VA. They knew each other. Would it be one of them?

She took out her phone and ran down her contact list, jogging her memory. Ellen settled on three names, all of whom she thought Chernov was friends with and were still in the area.

She glanced at her watch. It was almost one AM. Not a great time to be calling people. But it couldn't be helped.

All three numbers had the same result. The calls were answered, two by the women from the therapy group, one by her husband who turned the phone over to his wife, all three said they remembered Ellen, all thought it was a good article, and none had heard from Chernov in about a month. Then they all politely said goodbye.

Ellen shook her head. Well, maybe it was good news. Maybe Chernov really was on her way to New England. She looked up to see Ross, still in front of Karen's door, motioning to her. She got up and quickly walked down the hall.

"Deevers is awake," Barrows said. "She asked for you. Go on in."

Ellen entered the room and saw JJ standing beside Karen, gently holding her hand.

"There she is," Karen said, sounding tired but making a small smile.

"You probably should go back to sleep," Ellen said. "OK for you to be awake?"

"The doctor," JJ said, "says people do this sometimes, wake up at odd hours after surgery. She'll probably go back to sleep in a while."

"Needed to know you were all right," Karen said.

121

"I'm fine," Ellen said and, on impulse, bent over the woman and kissed her cheek. "You scared the hell out of me," she said.

"You didn't seem scared," Karen said. "Where're Chernov and Sharon?"

"No one knows," Ellen said.

"She hasn't called you?"

"No. Maybe she thinks I screwed things up?"

"Well, you are a reporter, but I don't think so. I think she's burrowed in somewhere, with another friend." She yawned. "My memories are a little scrambled but I think you went outside with my gun in your hand."

"I brought it back."

"Annie fucking Oakley." She yawned again. "I think I'm going to get a little more sleep now."

As Ellen watched, Karen's breathing became more pronounced and her head turned away. JJ reached over and turned out the light.

"No telling when she'll wake up again," he said, his voice low. "There's not a lot of sense in you hanging around here. I can give you a call later if you want."

"The doctor says everything is in the green?"

"Absolutely," JJ said. His eyes showed his relief. "She's totally out of the woods now. I'll be here."

"All right," she said. She reached over and squeezed his arm. "As long as you're here." She turned and left the room.

On her way out, she stopped to mention that Chernov had worked for Lowenstein. Ross seemed interested, though Barrows seemed too tired for things to register.

"We'll check it out," he said. "Remember: off the record for now."

"I'll be talking to you," Ellen said, grinning as she turned to walk away.

"Threat or promise?" Ross said to her back.

Ellen made no response as she walked down the hall but she raised her hand and wiggled her fingers. She nodded to the FBI agent standing outside the elevator and had a short wait until the doors slid open.

It had been a long day and the drive back to Philadelphia was going to be a challenge. Ellen smiled to herself; she stayed awake behind the wheel by singing along with tunes from her iPod, a practice that removed all doubt that she would never win a Grammy.

As the elevator arrived at the ground floor, another name, a friend of Chernov's from the therapy group, popped into her head. She checked her cell phone and found the name she remembered: Hannah O'Bannon.

There were two more police officers outside the elevator, both from the Chester County Sheriff's Service. One had a cup of coffee in his hand and both nodded to her. She punched in O'Bannon's number.

It was picked up as she approached the doors to the parking lot. Another county deputy and a woman wearing an FBI windbreaker were there.

"This is Ellen Parker," she said as she leaned against the door. "Is this Hannah?"

"I have got to change my number," Hannah replied, laughing. "Don't go anywhere, lady. I've got someone who wants to talk to you." Ellen heard voices in the background as she stepped onto the sidewalk. Then Chernov spoke.

"Hey, there you are. Are you OK? How is Deevers?"

"I'm fine," Ellen said. She picked up her pace as she walked to her car. "I spoke to Karen a little bit ago. She's fine, no complications."

"Good news."

"Listen, we've got to bring you in."

"Happy to come but I want to make sure Sharon isn't in any danger when we stick our heads up. That last thing…"

"I know, I know." Ellen shook her head. "I don't know how that happened."

"I think they had inside information."

"Really?"

"Hey, I'm paranoid but not stupid. A guy I used to work with, Don Brunner, I was in contact with him. I think he told…"

"You worked with Brunner as in when you were with New Joyton police?"

"Yes. Why?"

"I think I saw him," Ellen said, stopping in the middle of the deserted street. "Saw him? Where?"

"On the same floor as Karen. Listen, I'm going to hang up for a second and talk to the guys guarding her. I'll call you back in a minute, OK?"

"Absolutely. Shit."

Ellen realized as she broke the connection, she did not have either Barrows or Ross's numbers but did have Karen's. She turned back towards the hospital as she tried it, hoping JJ would hear it and pick it up.

A hundred feet away, John and Books saw her turn around.

"She's going back," Books said and John raised an eyebrow. "Do you want to grab her?"

"No," John said. "There's an unmarked car over there. See the bumper guards and the little things on the roof? Cop. I can't tell if anyone is in it or not."

"Right. She's going in." Books leaned back in his seat. "Now what do we do?"

"What we do best. Wait." John smiled as if aware of a joke that he got but Books didn't.

Books nodded but said nothing.

JJ picked up the phone as Ellen entered under the gaze of the two deputies. She paused.

"Hello," he said.

"JJ, it's Ellen."

"What's up?"

Ellen explained what she had seen and told Barrows and Ross about.

"What I just found out from Beth is that the cop she thinks leaked information about where she was is someone she knows. His name is Don Brunner. Can you tell Ross and Barrows?"

"Don Brunner, got it," JJ said. "Hold on." There came muffled sounds while Ellen stood waiting. Then Barrows came on the phone.

"Ellen, Agent Barrows. Chernov identified the New Joyton officer she thinks passed information to the people at the pizza place?"

"Yes. His name is Don Brunner. She worked with him back when she was in their police department, so I guess it was natural for her to contact him when she was trying to bring in Sharon Stuart."

"I understand. Hold on a second." She heard Barrows talking, passing Brunner's name, and then he came back. "There's a lot going on and this piece fits some other ones. I'm going to give you my and Ross's cell numbers. Can you copy?"

"Yes," Ellen said as she pulled a small pad out of her coat pocket. Barrows gave her the numbers.

"I'm going to turn you over to JJ," Barrows said. "Listen, it's very important for Chernov to bring the kid in."

"I understand."

"She trusts you," Barrows said, unknowingly echoing John's judgment. "Set it up. We'll cooperate and come get her or she can come to us. The longer she's out there, the greater the chance this guy is going to find her. I'm not talking about Brunner now. Brunner, I think, was just a scout. The guy I'm talking about is the man we're off the record about, right? He's worse than the people at the pizza place, a lot worse."

"I'm working on it now," Ellen said. "I'll be calling her back in a moment."

"Great. Here's JJ."

More sounds of the phone being passed and then JJ's deep voice came on.

"I heard," he said. "Here's my cell number." He slowly recited the numbers and Ellen added them to her list.

"I wish I could lend a hand," JJ said. "But I've got to stay with Karen."

"Of course," Ellen said. "Not a problem. If she wakes up before I get back, say hello for me."

"My turn to say 'of course,'" JJ said. "Watch your back."

Ellen nodded to the deputies, and for the second time walked out of Brandywine Hospital. She took a breath and called Hannah again.

"What's the deal?" Chernov asked.

"I passed on your information about Brunner," Ellen said. She glanced up at the sky and saw nothing. The hospital lights blotted out the stars.

"Good, I think," Chernov said.

"Now, about you and Sharon," Ellen said. "The FBI guy, Special Agent Barrows, said they would come to you or you could come on in."

"Yeah, well…" Ellen heard Chernov let out a sigh. "Yeah, I know we have to come in. I'm just really antsy about running into trouble, you know?"

Ellen nodded silently. Chernov, she knew, had been through a lot. Her deployments, combat, and then the rape, what the shrinks called 'Military Sexual Trauma.' It had taken her time to get things straight and it hadn't been easy.

"You still there, Ellen?"

"Yes. Listen, I am not trying to scare you but I think you need to know what is going on."

"Well," Chernov said, "you just scared the hell out of me." She did not sound scared but a little amused.

"The people looking for you," Ellen said, "have brought in a guy, a real bad guy." She paused. "Listen, I'm not supposed to say too much. This is all on background."

"I'm not planning on putting anything on Wikileaks," Chernov said.

"This guy, they think he may be a serial killer."

Chernov said nothing for a heartbeat.

"One good deal after another," she said finally. "I think I'm going to have to borrow some of Hannah's guns."

"Beth, I'm not kidding."

"Neither am I. All right, here is what we do. I'm not going to wake up Sharon to go driving off into the night. I want to be able to see what we're doing."

"How about if I have the FBI guys come to you?"

"No, we'll come to them. The less chatter there is among the police, the less likely Brunner and anyone else like him will hear it and try to get to us first." Her voice was touched by anger and Ellen wondered if it was about Brunner's betrayal of her or of just being a cop.

"Understood. How about if I come over to you? I've got Hannah's address."

"Sure, that would be fine. Be careful when you knock, though. Hannah's got that PTSD you've heard so much about and may throw the couch at you."

"Wow," Ellen said, smiling, "a sort of joke."

"Sort of. She wouldn't really; Sharon's asleep on it. Be careful."

"What could possibly go wrong at this point?"

Ellen heard Chernov's laughter as she broke the connection. She put her phone away and walked to her car.

It was a little weird, but it seemed to her the more dangerous things got, the more, what was the word she wanted?, the more at ease Chernov became. It was as if it was a state she was more comfortable with than ordinary living.

What did you have to encounter in your life to be like that? Ellen made a half smile. She had a good idea what the answer was.

"There she is," Books said. "Making a phone call."

The woman seemed to taking the whole night with her call and Books frowned. The police had not yet begun checking out the cars in the parking area but it was just a matter of when they would secure the inside of the

126

hospital and then come outside, looking for someone stupid enough to be hanging around.

Finally, Ellen Parker put her phone away and walked to her car. He reached to start but John touched his hand.

"Not yet," John said. "It's a long driveway they have. Wait until she's well along it. This time of night, we won't have any trouble following her. She can see our lights, so hang way back."

"Got it," Books said and withdrew his hand.

"All right, she's rolling. Don't start until she's down the drive."

"Right, got it," Books said, feeling a flash of irritation. He watched as Parker drove past the visitors' long parking lot. She passed the employees' lot, now mostly empty, and waited until her brake lights came on as she reached the intersection for the main road.

Books started up and eased out of their space and carefully made his way to the drive.

"She's signaling left turn," John said. "There she goes. Nice and steady."

Books reached the intersection and stopped for the red light. He twisted his neck and saw her brake lights flare again.

"She's getting on 30 by-pass," Books said. "Westbound. Not to Philly. She's going to the kid."

"She may not get on the by-pass, she may be taking the road past it."

The light turned green and Books quickly pulled out; he wanted to see Parker turn. He hated admitting it but John was right about the road. It continued past the hard-right turn onto the westbound lane of US 30 and she might be following it.

The four-lane by-pass always had some traffic on it, even at one in the morning. He saw her turn off the road onto the entrance ramp and then she disappeared behind a tall, highway maintenance shed. He saw her merging into very light traffic.

"Not too close," John said.

"No shit."

Books made the sharp turn onto the ramp and another sharp turn into the merge. He did not have to deal with any traffic and ahead by a little more than half a mile were the lights of her car. She was passing some kind of truck, almost invisible in the darkness except for its lights.

She really was going to the kid. Books smiled; the money was almost in sight.

"That truck will block our view of her," John said, "but if she goes for an exit, we'll see her. In the meantime, she can't see us. Good position, nice job."

"Thanks," Books said. He wondered if John was being sarcastic and then realized he didn't care. He was along for the ride to the money. After that, goodbye Dr. John. Hell, maybe he would go to Florida – Tallman wouldn't think of looking for him there.

He smiled. It was a dumb idea. Better to head west. He knew some people working the Tennessee-Kentucky line moving weed, the biggest cash crop south of the Ohio River. They were always looking for people.

Books glanced at John. The man was leaning against the door window, waiting for Parker to go for an exit. Getting the hell away from that nutcase would be a good first move.

An idea formed. If half the money was good, was not all the money better? *Two in the head.*

Chapter 17

Ellen's lips and hands were tight. She had seen the lights of a car follow her away from the hospital and get onto 30 behind her. She almost was certain. Almost.

Maybe it was nothing; maybe she was catching some of Beth's paranoia. Maybe she just needed some sleep. She shook her head.

There was nothing wrong with checking it out. As she drove through the night, Ellen put together a plan.

She knew the bypass and the business version of 30 merged together several miles ahead. A few miles beyond that was the small town of Gap. A shopping center, garages, fast food places, and gas stations lay scattered around. All right, she would stop for gas. That would give her a chance to carefully check to see if she was really being followed.

If there was any hint at all, she would call every cop she could. If not, fine, continue on down the road until she came to the intersection that would take her to O'Bannon's apartment building.

Having a plan under her control gave her a sense of security and she smiled at herself. A plan? The best laid plan…

Ellen checked her mirrors when the highway curved. The truck she passed was almost a mile behind her and between it and her was the car she had seen.

Or thought she had seen.

She resisted the impulse to press the accelerator. She doubted her little Toyota could outrun much and assumed that any bad guys would be driving a car capable of outrunning her. Better to not give them any reason to think she suspected them. Besides, racing on US 30 at night was an unpleasant way to be introduced to some of the local deer.

The miles passed and soon Ellen was off the four lane and merged onto the business branch. Now they were down to three lanes. Ellen stayed at the speed limit and the car behind her kept its distance.

It did not turn away, just kept following.

She came over a hill and descended rapidly into Gap. Ahead she saw lights, but most were for businesses that were closed. A gas station just before a major intersection caught her eye and she turned in.

Behind her, the car that she thought followed her drove on past, not slowing down. As she got out of her car, Ellen watched it, trying for its license plate but saw nothing other than its Pennsylvania colors.

The car kept going and then slowed, its turn signal coming on. Another truck almost blocked her view but she saw it turn onto a cross route, one of the innumerable country roads that meandered along ancient cow paths among the farms at the edge of Chester and Lancaster Counties.

All that for nothing, she thought. Ellen reached back into the car and flipped the lever to open the gas panel. Might as well do something constructive.

"Go," John said, but, where someone else might have yelled it, he just said it. "Turn up ahead to the right."

Books understood what John wanted to do. If they could circle around, they could come up on the gas station from the east and return to following the woman.

"I think she's made us," John said.

Books did not know what John based his idea on but he remained focused on driving.

He took the turn almost too fast but he had control. He accelerated coming out of the turn and hit his brights. Up ahead, the reflecting red octagon of a stop sign glowed. Books disregarded the injunction and again took the turn as fast as he could. As the car straightened, he could see US 30 ahead of them, their loop almost complete.

Now, if only she was still there…

Ellen put the nozzle back and tightened down her cap. As she slapped the panel closed, she glanced inside the gas station. They advertised hot coffee and she smiled. Maybe a large one to go would free up some of her brain cells.

Ellen walked in to the sound of an electronic bell chiming and nodded at the woman behind the counter, who barely looked up from her laptop as she wrote notes on a small pad.

She went to the back and poured herself the largest coffee she could and spent a minute finding the right size lid. She looked around and saw nothing else inviting.

Ellen paid the woman, interrupting her fixation on her computer.

"School?" she asked, nodding at the laptop.

"Intro biology," the woman said as she gave Ellen her change. She smiled a little, exposing a bright white smile that contrasted with her brown skin. "How could you tell?"

"Been there, done that," Ellen said, grinning. She raised her cup in a toast and went outside.

The coffee was hot enough that it made her hand uncomfortable and she passed it to her other hand. She walked around her car and fished for her keys.

Pain struck her; unfocused, it seemed everywhere. It seemed to fill her entire body, immobilizing her, as if every muscle was under another brain's control. She knew she was falling but could not even put a hand out to break her fall. She wanted to cry out but could not. Then it stopped and she tried to move.

Hands grabbed her, forcing her own hands back, pinning her on the ground. Something was slapped across her mouth. A car pulled up and the hands pulled her to the other side of the pumps. She was pushed into the back. The door slammed shut as her ankles were bound by something thin and tight. She struggled and felt the thin restraints bite into her wrists and ankles.

Someone was sitting beside her and, in the midst of her pain and terror, she felt her head being stroked.

"There, there," he said and covered her eyes with the same tape covering her mouth. "It won't be long now."

The woman studying course work on her laptop smiled as she finally understood a part of her reading assignment and instinctively looked out toward the fuel pumps, wondering if the thin white woman had left yet.

What she saw froze her in place for a second and may have saved her life. On the other side of the pumps from Ellen's car she saw a gray sedan, its back door open, while a man wearing glasses pushed a woman wearing the same slacks as her customer into the car.

The woman's wrists crossed behind her. The man's jacket had ridden up, exposing a handgun in the small of his back.

"Sweet Mother of God," she said and, as the car door slammed shut, she did the bravest thing she had ever done. Though scared, she ran out from

131

behind the counter and shoved open the glass door. She skidded to a halt as the gray car made a small bounce, lunging onto 30, and raced away into the darkness. She saw only the first three letters of the license plate.

Reciting the letters over and over as she ran back to the counter, she pulled a page from her notepad and wrote them down. Then she picked up her phone and hit the speed dial.

"Chester County Nine One One. What is your emergency?"

John looked back at the gas station and glimpsed a woman standing near the pumps but she turned and ran back into the building. Of course she ran away, he thought. That's how they were, totally helpless in an emergency. He grinned in the darkness of the backseat; everything was going right, as if it was preordained.

Books kept his speed to within the legal limit and waited for John to tell him when to turn. John kept looking back, waiting until they were out of sight of the gas station, turning back only to adjust his grip on the squirming woman.

"If you want to be Tasered again," John said, "keep giving me a hard time." The squirming stopped.

"Take the next right," John said, and Books carefully took the car onto what appeared to be a two-lane farm road. "It's going to be around fifteen minutes. Just keep going north."

Books had no idea where they were but John had told him he had a place, a "private place," in the north part of the county. They would need privacy to find out where the hell the money was. Beyond that, Books was not letting himself think.

But the thoughts he held just out of sight were as dark as the Pennsylvania night they ran through.

Twenty-two minutes after her abduction, the car containing Ellen Parker stopped momentarily. The man who held her moved, pushing her as he leaned forward.

"That one," he said. "The one next to the ignition key. Right, that one."

The car's engine stopped and the driver got out of the car. Ellen heard little that made sense except for a faint squeal of metal. The driver got back into the car and they pulled forward.

"Lock it up," the man holding her said.

"All right," the driver said. He sounded like he resented being ordered. The car stopped with the engine still running. The driver got out but didn't bother to close his door.

The squeak came again and this time she heard what sounded like a chain pulled through a gate.

The car pulled forward an unknown distance, but it did not run long before it stopped and they dragged her out of the car. Her eyes taped, she saw nothing as the two men carried her across gravel.

They carried her up wooden steps and then paused, laying her on a plank porch. She could smell pine, faint in the cool night air.

A door opened and she was lifted and carried inside.

"Not here," the man said. "In back."

Another door opened. This room was unheated and almost immediately they stopped. She was dropped onto a springless bed with a thin mattress.

"All right," the man said. For a moment, he remained silent and Ellen had the feeling he was looking at her, savoring his capture. Then he stepped forward.

She was rolled onto her side, her hands were freed, only to be immediately reattached to the head of the bed. Then the thin strip holding her ankles together was cut free – she felt the knife blade – and the man's hands jerked open her slacks and pulled at her waist.

Ellen raised both knees as hard as she could, hitting the man in his side. It was not a very powerful blow but he grunted as if it had hurt. For a second, a fierce joy competed with her terror, and then the man slapped her in the side of her head.

She almost lost consciousness and her ear rang with a high-pitched howl that sounded like it was not going to go away. Something had scratched her with his slap but the blow itself provided pain and it seemed to increase for several seconds.

Ellen felt something sharp touch her neck and she willed herself to hold as still as her heartbeat would allow. It hurt and it slowly rotated. She felt a drop of blood crawl down her neck.

"Do I have your attention, bitch?" He peeled the tape off her eyes.

The room she was in was poorly lit by a single small lamp. The talking man stood over her, in every way ordinary, average, except his eyes. Flat eyes looked at her through glasses with as little emotion as a shark might show.

133

Behind the flat-eyed man was another, but her focus was on him. She clenched her jaw and said nothing.

"I think I do," he said. He seemed amused.

The knife point did not go away but his free hand went back to her trousers. He pushed them down, along with her panties, awkwardly using just one hand.

"My name," he said, "is Doctor John." He smiled and cocked his head as he looked at her. "The Night Tripper, right? You get it?" John studied her face and then shrugged.

"First thing I want to do," John said, "is impress upon you the need to cooperate."

The knife went away. He used both hands to drag her trousers and panties off. Then he pushed her shirt and bra up.

"A little on the thin side," he said. He took off his glasses and carefully put them aside.

This isn't about me, she told herself. Ellen made herself focus on everything she had heard from the women with Elizabeth Chernov, from Beth herself, about being raped.

This is what he is, not me. I did nothing to deserve this. He's the asshole.

The pain, driving, tearing, came and she felt tears form. She remembered what they, the women, said and she clenched it with her heart and soul.

Stay alive. Whatever it takes. This is not about me. When this is over, I will leave it here and move on.

John stuck his tongue in her ear as if he wanted her aroused. He slammed into her as if he wanted her broken.

Stay alive. This says nothing about me. Stay alive and live to see him face down in the dirt.

Then he was done.

"Oops," John said and she heard the smile. "Made a bit of a mess." Ellen opened her eyes to see him adjusting his glasses, still looking very ordinary except for the eyes that lacked a soul. He paused, noticing her looking at him and then turned to the other man. "You want some of this?"

"No, man," the other man said. "I'm not into greasy seconds." John laughed and pushed his glasses higher onto the bridge of his nose.

"All right, you can go first next time."

Thirty-seven minutes after Ellen Parker's abduction, Phillip Ross's cell phone buzzed. As he was told what had happened, he reached out and grabbed

Agent Barrows' shoulder. Like Ross, Barrows slouched almost asleep in the waiting room near Deever's room while their relief maintained the guard in front of her door.

"All right," he said and Barrows, noticing something in his tone, straightened in his chair. He waited while Ross put away his phone.

"Ellen Parker," Ross said, "has been abducted. She stopped for gas in Gap." Seeing Barrows' eyebrows go up, he explained. "Major road intersection just inside Lancaster County. Eye witness saw at least one man pull her into another car and got a partial on the license plate. State police picked up the call. They ran her plate, her car was left at the scene, and called her residence. Answering machine gave her name and work number as an alternative. News reporter thing."

"Is this our guy, you think?"

"I think we have to assume it is. She's a person he might go after to find out where Chernov and the little girl are." He paused. "And, she's a woman."

"God damn it," Barrows said as he got to his feet. "You let the state police know what we are concerned with. I'm calling the task force."

"I got it," Ross said.

Forty minutes after Ellen Parker's abduction, Books stood outside the cabin and looked up at the invisible sky. It smelled like rain.

What the hell was wrong with Doctor John? Since the rape, he had done nothing, just sat looking at Parker. When Books suggested getting to asking some questions, John had just waved his hand.

"She'll tell us everything," he said. "They always do."

Books could all but hear a ticking clock. Somewhere out there in the dark, small hours, a ton of cops were looking for them. This was not what he wanted. He wanted some money and a head start on Tallman before some of his people not prone to making use of Miranda warnings showed up.

They would know he was with the Doctor. Someone probably had been to the garage already. People like Bobby Jacks would be looking and they would start with whoever Tallman had gone through to get Doctor John.

Doctor John...

John was different. He wasn't like anyone Books had ever met. He had known killers hot and cold but John did not seem to be interested in money or business or anything other than inflicting terror.

135

John had said he wanted Books to survive because when he left, it would draw away the police. But Books suspected that the recovery of the money, which he needed to go anywhere, was something that John really didn't care about. That thought tossed a cupful of kerosene on the fire rolling around in Books' mind.

And what John cared about was a woman tied down on the frame of a bed. So much so that he seemed to be losing track of the swarm of cops they had provoked.

All right, they seemed to be safe in this compound, whatever it was. Books looked around. Most of the buildings had small lights over doorways but some did not, suggesting maintenance was not a priority. It resembled one of those commercial hunting camps that nestled up next to state game lands. There were ten or so cabins, at least two longer buildings that extended off into the darkness, and a large, central building with two pick-up trucks parked outside. It had some kind of crude cross hammered to the wall. A church?

It made no sense that they were hiding on the grounds of some religious outfit and Books was not eager to look into John's flat eyes to ask what was going on.

John came out onto the porch and stretched.

"We're going to get to the questions in a few minutes." He smiled. "If you want some of her, now would be the time."

"No, but thanks." Books looked out into the dark. "I'm thinking we should be moving on."

"No problem. I'll have her talking quick."

"What will we do with her then?"

"Leave her," John said. "I'm not coming back here. Sort of a going away gift. Be back in a minute. Need to get some things."

John stepped off the porch and walked away.

Books watched him for a moment and then entered the cabin. He did not want to but he went to the back room.

Parker was still tied to the bed frame. She was awake and had been crying but she showed nothing as he looked at her.

Tough bitch. Books saw John's jacket hanging on the chair he had sat on while watching her.

Glancing over his shoulder, he put his hand into the jacket. He found the folded envelope with papers inside. He pulled it out and quickly looked at the papers.

The first one was a list of names. His name was on the list.

Books folded the papers and put them back into the envelope. He put it back in the jacket and looked up to see Ellen Parker staring at him.

Almost involuntarily, he looked behind him as he drew his pistol. John had not returned. He looked at Parker and a thought came to him.

Two in the head.

Fifty-one minutes after Ellen Parker's abduction, John paused in the cabin used for holding maintenance equipment. He thought he heard a car but, as he listened, there was nothing. He shrugged and went back to putting interesting items into a small toolbox. A moment later, he walked back to his cabin with a smile on his face.

John had two reasons to smile. First, of course, there was the hour ahead he was going to spend with Ellen Parker. While he would like to take more time with the young woman, the reality was time was becoming short.

The other reason he smiled was he had solved a problem.

Yes, he would ask Parker questions. Who knew, maybe he could use the information to recover the money the little girl carried. Then he would go to Idaho.

But that would take time and John already knew Parker would not cooperate. She would not bargain. He had learned that during the rape. She had been terrified but her eyes showed something else and, whatever it was, it did not put her into the category of women who would try to cooperate for their lives.

She reminded him of the blond, the last woman he had left hanging on the wire. John smiled slightly; his ribs still ached, but, when he was done and before he left, he would leave Parker on the chain link fence of the compound as a gift for the reverend.

After all, thinking of Donaldson had solved his problem. He could take his time with Parker and still leave with a pile of money even if he couldn't get to Sharon Stuart.

He could take Donaldson's. The thought made him smile as he stepped up onto the porch. The reverend did not realize that John had been in his office several times and, being a thorough person, had found the false bottom to a desk drawer.

It was filled with money, more than the $25,000 he had been promised if he killed everyone on the list. John nodded as he walked through the cabin.

Finish with Parker, leave his present to Donaldson, take the money, and, yes, he had not forgotten, kill Books. Then leave.

John stepped into the back room, a smile already on his face, and saw the empty bed.

Fifty-one minutes after Ellen Parker's abduction, Books eased the car into gear and rolled down the hill to the compound gate. While John had heard the car start, the bulk of the hill blocked the sound of the car's movement.

At the gate, Books, using the keys John had left in the car, opened the lock and pushed open the gate. Back in the car, he started the car again and drove down the sloping road.

He looked behind him as he left, expecting to see an outraged John chasing after him. But there was no one in his rear-view mirror.

John had told him that he wanted Books to serve as a distraction to the police once he took off. That was a lie – his name was at the top of the list. But it was not a bad plan. Books nodded; John could be clever.

Thing was, Books could be clever, too. He had taken John's plan and reversed it. He would get away from John and John would have to deal with a distraction.

Ellen Parker.

Sure, he could have tried to kill John, but Books realized there was something very dangerous about John, dangerous in a way that did not match any of the very dangerous people he had known while working for Tallman.

So he decided he would kill John if he had to make the attempt, but it was far easier to just leave.

And leave John with something to occupy his time and maybe serve as a distraction for the police. That's why he had cut the plastic strips holding Parker's wrists to the bedframe.

She had said nothing when he told her to take off. Parker had just laid there for a moment, probably trying to put everything together. Finally, she sat up.

"I'm out of here," Books had said. "I suggest you be the same way. Run." Then he turned and walked out of the room. As he stepped off the steps, he heard the soft patter of Parker's feet, running behind him. He heard her running for a few strides on the gravel and then there was nothing.

Books congratulated himself. One problem was solved; he had gotten away from Doctor John and he suspected there were very few people who could say that.

He still had the problem of how to get away from Tallman. Well, there was a way to solve that problem, an idea that had come to him from that same article that discussed ways of breaking into middle management. Sometimes a problem could be made into an opportunity.

Books smiled. That article was full of good ideas.

Fifty-one minutes after her abduction, Ellen Parker stood in darkness at the base of a chain link fence and realized she did not have the strength to climb it. The fence's inter-locking steel wire offered finger grips but it would be impossible to get more than toeholds for her feet.

Somewhere behind her was a serial killer who, by now, had to know she was gone.

What kind of game was the other man playing? She had seen him read the papers belonging to the killer. His eyes had gone wide and then narrowed as he read and were still narrow as he put the papers and their envelope back.

He had looked at her and she knew that he was also a dangerous man, but not in the same way as the killer.

When he walked to her and took out his small pocket knife, Ellen had felt cold panic squeeze her heart. Cutting her free was incomprehensible. Telling her to run almost froze her in place with its unexpected impact.

As he had walked away, Ellen had stood, swaying slightly, physically exhausted and feeling slow drops of blood run down her thighs. She pulled on her clothes, her arms leaden, her fingers almost numb and barely responsive, everything coming to life slowly as she struggled with her shoes.

She ran past him, fully expecting him to turn and shoot her. It was only when her feet hit the ground that she realized he had given her a chance to live for reasons unknown. Ellen turned sharply, gambling that going behind the cabin would put it between her and the men.

Then she had found the fence. Its posts were set in concrete and strips of steel ran from pole to pole, anchoring the fence at the bottom. At the top, horizontal poles attached to each post and were wired into the chain link. Ten feet high, some kind of looping wire was at the top.

Ellen reached up and grabbed the fence. The wire bit into her hands. Her body felt like it had been drained of control and strength by the rape.

Impossible.

She pulled with both arms, bringing her face up to her hands while her feet pawed at the fence. Ellen dropped down, her fingers raw, her eyes still on the fence.

She licked her lips. She was afraid and remembered being afraid in the past. Part of her wanted to run away, to find another way.

"Screw it," she whispered.

Ellen reached up again and gripped the fence. The wire felt worse against her fingers. She raised her feet slowly and deliberately did not allow herself to thrash. She pressed, searching for the openings in the fence, seeking enough purchase for the toe of her shoes.

She found it. Steadied by her toes, she released one hand and reached up and gripped the fence. The pain in her hand blossomed. Ellen carefully brought up her other hand and clenched her fingers around the wire.

Her raw fingers hurt to hold onto the fence but when she brought up her first foot they seemed to explode in pain. Ellen found a toe hold and raised the other foot.

Her anchored foot slipped out and her whole weight was held by her burning hands. She felt her feet moving like she was on a bike, so rapidly did they search for a hold.

Ellen stopped her legs and forced herself to concentrate on each foot, carefully raising them, keeping her toes pointed at the fence, and then gently forcing them into the narrow gaps in the woven wire.

Slowly using her legs, she raised herself until her head again was even with her hands. Then Ellen raised her hands again.

She found the top bar but found also a curl of barbed wire. Ellen grabbed the cross pipe, trying to get her fingers between the braided ends of the fence wire. They scratched her wrists but it was a better grip than the wire had been.

Ellen pulled herself up, letting her feet come free and begin their slow and careful dance with the fence. She kept pulling and felt the first touch of the barbed wire.

It wasn't barbed wire. It was a steel ribbon, notched on both sides of its length to produce what felt like the sharp tips of knives. As Ellen pulled herself up, she entered into the loop of the wire.

She tried to push herself up so the cross pipe was at her waist but the sharp wire, which she remembered was called razor wire, caught her head and shoulders. The points stabbed her shoulders and she felt one cut deep into her scalp.

The wire was not a simple spiral as it journeyed across the top of the fence; it seemed to loop back onto itself, making shoving the loops aside impossible. Short, twisted lengths of steel wire anchored it to the top pole. Ellen managed to hold onto the cross pipe and press against it breast high. Everything from the cross pipe up was confronted by the wire.

She could not go through it. The self-connecting loops were like lassoes. The only thing was to go over it. Ellen thought about trying to take off her coat and lay it on top of the razor wire like a blanket but time was short.

Ellen, holding tightly to the cross pipe with her left hand, leaned back, released her right hand, and then flashed on an old John Wayne movie as she arced her arm up and forward.

"Forward, ho," she whispered through clenched teeth. She pressed down with her arm and felt the razor wire sag while, at the same time, it slashed her forearm. She pushed down harder and pulled herself to the cross pipe. Ellen felt the wire stab into her breasts and stomach as she raised herself and then lay on top of the razor wire.

Her hips were on the cross pipe and she leaned forward, trying to roll over the razor wire while both hands, now slick with blood and weak from exertion, tried to control her movement.

Ellen's right hand slipped and she fell, only to be jerked to a painful halt as the razor wire, as if determined not to allow her to escape, grabbed at her body and held her suspended ten feet above the ground.

She hung on the wire, her body in agony, and she knew John would find her there.

He would.

"No," Ellen said, but there had not been a question that anyone else could have heard. "No," and she used her free hand to push the wire away from her pinned arm. While her trailing leg was snared, she lifted her other leg up, brought it next to the trapped leg, and then lowered it, pushing the razor wire down.

She knew from the sudden sag that she was free. All she had to do was roll and fall into the dark, fall ten feet to the ground she could not see.

Ellen took a breath, closed her eyes, and rolled, trying to get her legs under her. She almost succeeded but slammed into the ground hard enough to knock the wind out of herself.

It was more than a minute before she could breathe, though pain sat on her as if it had no intention of leaving soon. Ellen got herself to her hands and knees, looked back at the dimly lit compound, and then downhill into the dark of the surrounding forest. She crawled for the first three feet because that was all she could do. Then she got to her feet. She could feel blood oozing down her body from the rape, fence, and razor wire but it did not matter.

Nothing else mattered. She was alive.

Chapter 18

Sergeant Donald Brunner felt his world collapsing. Being required to check the hospital for Tallman's person was dangerous enough exposure – he had the feeling he had pushed things very far, perhaps too far. There had only been State Police and county deputy sheriff uniforms in the hospital and he only barely had managed to keep from being spotted. Even some woman in a waiting area had looked at him as if he was something unusual.

All right, that was probably just paranoia, but there was no question Beth Chernov had reason to think he was not just another officer in a small-town police force. Once she told her story, people would have very tough questions for him.

What he needed was information and the best place for it was the New Joyton Police Department. If he could tap into law enforcement communications, he could learn if Chernov was still on the loose or, preferably, dead or, far worse, blabbing her damned head off to the County Sheriff.

It was all Chernov's fault, anyway. As screwed up in her head as she was, what the hell was she doing riding to the rescue of that kid?

Concentrating on the answer to his question distracted Brunner enough that he did not realize that he almost had pulled into the parking area for New Joyton Borough Services, including police. Parked in front of him were two Pennsylvania State Police cars; behind them was a dark car and Brunner knew it was from the same agency. All three cars had brought those people with the tough questions.

Brunner drove past, glad he was in his own car but wishing he was not in his sergeant's uniform.

Now what?

He had money; Tallman had been generous for services rendered and Brunner had been careful not to flash it around or make any unusually large deposits. Almost all of it was in two suitcases in a self-storage facility near Exton, almost on the other side of the county from New Joyton.

Getting to it might be a challenge. If they were looking for him, then his car was identified. He needed help.

He thought of Mr. Tallman.

Doctor John, as he liked to think of himself, stood for a moment staring at the empty bed, his lips tight. He felt betrayed, as if something unfair had been done to him. He stepped toward his jacket and felt his shoe slip.

It was blood. She left a blood trail.

"Did I bust your cherry, little girl?" John asked, pulling on his jacket. Then, as he followed the scattered droplets, shook his head. No woman was a virgin, they were all whores. He had learned that as a boy, a history that on rare occasions – rare any more – still returned in his dreams.

She had gotten what she deserved, there was no question of that. And she deserved much, much more. Especially for running away.

Where was Books?

Had she done something to Books? He shook his head. That was impossible. So why was Books not here?

John's head turned almost robot-like towards Reverend Donaldson's office at the rear of the chapel. That was where the money was.

He ran off the cabin steps, all the way to the office. The door was locked but John did not pause. Rage powered the foot he used to kick open the door and then he was inside, clawing at the drawer with a hammer from the toolbox he still carried.

The drawer took longer than the door but it came free. John pulled out the papers in it and threw them to one side, forced himself to slow down so he could find the correct spot to press, and pulled away the false bottom.

The drawer was empty, the money gone. John stared at it for a moment as his mind made connections driven by his dark needs. The money was gone. Parker was gone. Books was gone.

They were in it together.

He ran to the door and looked out. The car he had used was gone. Everything fit. John reached over to a small board where keys to the pick-ups hung. He grabbed a set and then ran back to the cabin, discarding the toolbox for a flashlight.

John followed the blood trail to the fence and smiled with grim satisfaction at the drops of red still glistening on the wire. All right, she was outside. She wasn't with Books – he felt disappointed – and so Books had to have the money.

Where would Books go? John needed money to get to Idaho – in Idaho everything would be perfect. He believed that, he needed to believe that, more than he believed the sun would rise in the next few hours.

The Reverend Donaldson probably didn't have any money left after Books' theft, John's logic told him, so there was no point in going after the minister, as enjoyable as that would be.

John shook his head as he walked back to the cabin. Books was probably running for his life. Maybe it was time he did the same thing.

He moved his bed and lifted a board from the floor. A small bag held John's money from his journey north. There wasn't much but it was better than nothing.

From a free-standing cupboard, John pulled out several shirts and a pair of slacks. They and some underwear went into a cloth laundry bag. Both bags went behind the driver's seat. He placed his tablet and graphic novel on the front seat.

Ellen Parker. He shook his head. She wasn't on Tallman's list but she should have been. He smiled, thinking of a line from a movie. Who was that masked man? Well, who was she? He brought the tablet to life and dropped her name into Google. Giving the glowing machine a moment to work its magic, he inserted the key to the ignition.

The truck started easily and John drove to the gate. It was open and he realized Books had unlocked it, using the keys from his car. John felt disappointed. Parker got away, Books got away, and the money, it was all very disappointing. Well, he knew one way to raise his spirits and once he got out of Pennsylvania he promised himself a major indulgence.

Or two.

When Ellen reached the trees, she stopped running, guessing that her noise would attract attention. She crouched, putting her hands on her thighs as she lowered herself behind a tree.

Up the hill, the compound still had a scattering of lights. Around her there was only darkness.

Then she heard a semi tractor-trailer behind her. Looking through the trees, she saw a flash of headlights.

She was close to a road, though she had no idea what road it was. Ellen started to rise and her hand touched her pants pocket.

She felt the shape of her cell phone. It could not possibly be, but it was. The men had not taken it. Was the one so taken by his need to hurt that he had stopped thinking? Maybe the other hadn't cared; she didn't know what the other man was about.

Ellen brought the phone to life and touched the map app. As she tried to walk quietly toward the road, the phone took several minutes before it showed her just off of Route 23.

Then she saw the low battery indicator. It started flashing and she knew she just had seconds.

She remembered a speed dial number and punched it in. The ringing tone came twice, three times, and Ellen wondered if anyone was going to pick up.

"Hello," Hannah O'Bannon said.

"It's Ellen. I'm just off the road on 23, north side, next to the game lands. I'm out of battery. Can you come and get me?"

There was no response. She looked at the display and, as she watched, it shut itself off.

She was alone.

John slammed on the brakes and quickly backed up the truck. Donaldson's money wasn't in the drawer. Where was it? He felt the need to know and that need had become more powerful as he had packed. Now, about to leave the compound, he had to respond to it.

With the truck tires throwing gravel as he traveled in reverse all the way back to Donaldson's office, John felt the need growing.

He ran into the office and then made himself stop. Yes, it was getting lighter outside and morning would be here in an hour or so but he had to look for it one more time.

He tore through the room, grabbing and tossing things, without quite realizing that what his real need was to destroy the office, a way of revenging himself on Donaldson. He pushed over a small sofa and cut the bottom out of it with his knife. Pictures on the wall sailed across the room and shattered against the other walls. A bookshelf, taller than he, came down, cascading political and religious books and pamphlets across the floor. John pulled up several throw rugs, looking for trap doors and hidden recesses.

146

The desk, the desk that had defied him and made him feel stupid, he saved for last. He pulled out all of the drawers and dumped what they had in a pile. Then, his rage peaking, he lifted the desk by one end and flipped it over, using strength even he had not imagined he had.

The desktop slammed into the floor, its crash only partly blocked by debris already there. John stepped up to it and kicked its side, doing little damage. He stepped back to kick again and looked down at his foot.

Beneath his foot, previously covered by the desk, several floor boards formed a perfect rectangle. John hesitated as if reluctant to give up the kick but he squatted down, his knife in his hand.

The knife was not needed; the boards were counter-balanced and, as he pushed at one end, they rotated smoothly upward. Lying in a lined cavity was a steel box, snug in its hiding place.

On top of the box was a pistol. John favored knives for important work but he was not one to pass up so obvious and useful a gift. He dropped the magazine and noted that it was full. He found a round in the chamber. How nice of the good reverend to leave him this parting gift; he regretted being unable to leave him the body of Ellen Parker, strung up on his fence and posing all sorts of difficult questions with the police. He shoved the pistol into his jacket pocket and then looked down at the box.

"You little bitch," John said, a grin appearing on his face. He wiped his mouth with one hand and picked up the box by a small handle on its top. He gently placed the box on the floor and then carefully undid its latches.

There was the money, surrendered, acknowledging his power and waiting for him because he deserved it.

Very slowly he closed the lid and snapped the latches shut. Had Donaldson discovered that John had searched his desk? It didn't matter. He, Doctor John the Night Tripper, had won. It didn't matter how much money it was. It wasn't about money; nothing John did was about money. Money was just a tool to get him to what mattered, and what mattered was he won.

He always won.

John took a moment to hug the small box to his chest, not realizing he made much the same gesture with many of his victims. Then he got to his feet and walked to the door. He turned and looked at the wreckage – not a piece of furniture was intact.

John could not resist the impulse. He put the box down, unzipped his jeans, and then urinated on the pile of books, paying particular attention to one with a swastika on its cover.

"Heil fucking Hitler," he said and laughed. These people were laughable – the only thing he had gotten from the white supremacists was an appreciation for the dramatic nature of their art work. Ever since encountering the double-lightning emblem of the SS, the *Schutzstaffel*, he had made a point, conditions permitting, to carve it into the thighs of his dead victims.

It was like branding. This one is mine. He nodded. These idiots thought he was a tool for them to use? They never understood they were his tools, his way of camouflaging himself. And when he left, they would be hunted by the mobs of police, all thinking they were acting like the Nazis they wanted to be.

It was very humorous, if you had a sense of humor, which most of them did not. He zipped up, looked around one more time and holding his box – and it was his, now and forever – close to his chest, John walked outside.

As he got into the truck, he saw the eastern sky was lighter. How long had he been inside? John glanced at his watch. Had it really been thirty minutes?

How time flies.

Then he remembered his tablet, glowing patiently on the seat beside him. John picked it up and was surprised at the first entry of the search engine. She was known to the Philadelphia Inquirer? He tapped the entry and read for a minute before shutting the device down.

"You can't make this stuff up," he said and smiled.

He started the truck and rolled out of the compound, already thinking about the best way to get onto the turnpike and calculating that he could be in Indiana by nightfall.

Elizabeth Chernov looked over her shoulder and saw that Sharon was still awake, though there was enough room in Hannah's extended cab pick-up for her to lie down.

"You don't want to go back to sleep?" she asked.

"No," Sharon said, looking out the side window. It was dark but light was slowly, almost reluctantly touching things. "I don't want to miss Ellen."

"Good idea," Chernov said. She turned around. "Are we close?"

"Just saw a game lands sign," Hannah said. "Should be somewhere in front of us. Slowing down."

"All right."

148

They were not sure if Ellen had heard Hannah's response. The connection had failed and they had not been able to raise her again. Both women refrained from discussing in front of Sharon why Ellen was out in the middle of what Chernov thought was a good definition for nowhere.

They knew nothing of the abduction or the police search for her. Agent Barrows' repeated calls to Chernov's cell phone had never gone through because, as if technology was in the mood to mock everyone this night, the phone's battery, like Ellen's, finally had failed.

If the idea was amusing, Chernov did not find it so. Something was very wrong. Part of it was they were slowing down. Back in "the sandbox," Iraq, slowing down was never a good idea. Bad things happened if they could get you to slow down.

Looking out her door window, Chernov smiled. Bad things happened even when you drove like a mad man. It was that kind of world.

"Got someone," Hannah said and Chernov jerked her head forward.

Ahead, just catching the furthest glow of their high beams, a figure stood by the road. Chernov resisted the urge to tell Hannah to speed up even as the other woman hit the gas and the truck lunged forward, pushing Chernov back into her seat and against the pistol in the small of her back.

It was almost over.

Doctor John followed the road down from the compound and coasted to a stop at the main road. He was careful to look both ways – now was not the time to get sloppy – and saw no one to the left. To the right he saw receding tail lights and guessed someone was really trying to get a jump on the commuter traffic this morning.

His GPS had an arrow to the right as the fastest way to the turnpike so John turned that way. The GPS was silent because he had turned off the woman's voice. Who was it who had thought men would want to be ordered around by a woman?

Ahead, the other vehicle seemed to have picked up speed. Probably familiar with the road. Route 23 was not terribly tricky but you either had to be alert in a few places or be one of the locals to go very fast on it.

Now the vehicle's brake lights were flaring to life. A deer cutting across the road? John slowed down. Getting involved in someone's accident was not something he wanted and he was considering, if the other vehicle had hit something, how he would turn around when he saw a figure in the headlights.

Ellen Parker.

Hannah skidded the truck to a halt half on the road's shoulder and then she and Chernov were out of the truck together. Chernov got to her first, even with taking a second to tell Sharon to stay in the truck. She wrapped Ellen in a hug and felt the woman's arms, at first weakly and then with gathering strength, return it. Hannah had one arm across Ellen's back but faced the dark trees, as if waiting for something to appear.

"What the fuck, lady?" Chernov finally asked, still holding onto Ellen but taking a half step back. A trail of blood ran down her face and Ellen's clothes were torn. There were blood stains everywhere, including between her legs. Chernov had a terrible flash of recognition but hoped what she thought wasn't true. "Where's your car?"

"Listen," Ellen said and her tone, angry, fearful, intense, had their attention immediately. "I was grabbed on my way to you. He wanted to find you and the money. He raped me. I escaped. We have to get out of here."

"Got it," Hannah said. "Beth, get her into the back. We're rolling." Her voice was matter of fact but emphatic, what you would expect to hear, Chernov decided, from a Marine sergeant in combat. As she assisted Ellen into the back, she was grateful that they weren't. They had enough to deal with without a war.

"Head for Brandywine Hospital," she said as she closed Ellen's door.

"Roger that," Hannah said. She had the truck moving before Chernov had her seat belt buckled.

John stopped and turned off his headlights when he saw two figures emerge from the truck ahead. Gripping the steering wheel, he almost bounced in his seat.

Parker had called for help, not from a bunch of heavily armed SWAT officers, but from a girlfriend. It was too ridiculous, too impossible. If there was a god, and John knew there was not, he had come down firmly on John's side.

Because women were just whores.

All right, now what? He had a chance – there was no question but he would take it. As he thought, he saw everyone get back into the truck. It looked like Ellen was moving slowly.

Served her right for taking off.

The truck started forward. He could force it off the road, take them into the forest, and do what needed to be done. As John thought, he eased his truck forward, his headlights still off. Forcing them off might be risky but...

The truck's brake lights came to life abruptly as the truck swerved off the road onto the shoulder and stopped. Doors opened as he approached and he saw Ellen emerge and take two steps before bending forward at the waist. Then she threw up.

John accelerated, swung to one side to avoid the truck, and then sharply cut in front of it, riding the brakes as it slowed to a halt on the shoulder.

"Hey, get out of the road!" he yelled as he got out, deliberately trying to confuse the women. "Are you having a problem?" The women looked at him, uncertain as to what had just happened, and Ellen, the betrayer, was slow to turn around as he walked around the front of his truck. As she saw him and terror began to touch her face, only then did he pull out his pistol.

It was all just too perfect, too wonderful. Three women.

He held the gun so that it was like how they did it in a movie he had seen, rolling his wrist to the left so the weapon was horizontal. It looked cool, professional. John moved it back and forth among the women.

And the little girl. A small head had appeared from the back of the cab. John smiled so broadly he felt his muscles stretch. This was all too, too perfect.

"Sharon Stuart, I believe," he said and the women looked back at the girl. "Well, don't just stand there, child. Bring your backpack and come on out." As the little girl slowly emerged, he stepped up to her and put his hand on her shoulder. Then he pointed with his pistol towards the woods.

"Everyone, let's take a walk into the trees," John said. He wanted to savor the moment but time was pushing him. How long would it be before someone drove and found the two trucks on the side of the road and called it in? He had to move quickly.

"And if we say no?" the tallest woman said.

"Then I start with the kid. Let's go."

The ground sloped upward but gently and the improving light helped everyone keep their footing. John walked at the rear of the group, one hand on Sharon and the strap to her backpack.

He heard the tall woman whisper something and Chernov's reply of, "Wait."

"No whispering," John said. "I might feel offended at being left out. And you don't want that."

It was a short distance to the trees and a few steps into them brought the group to a small clearing. Ellen led the small line and when John ordered everyone to stop, she took another step and then a small one, separating herself from the others. John took the backpack from Sharon and shoved her towards the women, then walked forward and faced the line.

"You have the money," Chernov said. "Take it and go. The longer you wait, the closer the police are coming." Her heart was pounding; the man had not searched them and the hard metal of the .45 pushed against her back. She would try but his gun was pointed at her…

Ellen knew what was coming. John would toy with them but, even in the dim light, she could see the contempt on his face, though no emotion touched his eyes. As John briefly looked into the backpack, she made another small step.

There was a chance, a pitifully small chance, Ellen thought, to save the others, especially Sharon. If she could get John to focus on her, the other women could grab Sharon and run off into the darkness of the forest. There was just a chance that the trees would protect them and John would not take the time to chase them down. Maybe.

If he was pointing away from them, if she charged him, that would distract him. And she would die. It did not seem to matter.

On the left of the line, Ellen stepped to her right, John's left, but his eyes were on Chernov.

"Well," John said, "let's agree that the police are coming somewhere, but not necessarily here. Right now, they are probably running in immense circles." He thought of Books and smiled. "But I do wish to be going. After all, what can you think of a state that has a place called 'Goosetown'?"

"What the hell are you talking about?" the tall woman asked.

"He's enjoying himself," Chernov said.

"Indeed," John said, unable to keep from prolonging his enjoyment. Oh, what he could do with three women if only there was time! Ellen took another step, moving further to his left but, though he noticed her move, he deliberately looked at Chernov. Let her think she had a chance. This was wonderful.

"I enjoyed reading about you, Ellen." Now his pistol swung towards her. He glanced at Chernov and the tall woman, both standing still, and then back at Ellen.

"Let the girl go," Ellen said. "You don't do kids." Was she far enough away to give them a chance?

"There's always a first time." John smiled, loving the moment.

"If you try to hurt her, I'll see you die."

"I believe you," John said. He looked back at Chernov and the tall woman. "She's a really dangerous woman. Did you know she killed a deputy sheriff? Very dangerous."

He looked back at Ellen, smiled, and fired.

The handgun, still horizontal, kicked back into John's hand but not severely. Ellen spun and collapsed, falling on her side. She lay still, partially curled, and John felt a growing glow inside him. It was not how he usually did it but it was, nonetheless, good. He looked back at the other two women.

They had guns in their hands raised so their eyes looked at him through their pistols' sights. He had time to feel a flash of fear and failure for not searching them as he tried to bring his gun around but the pain in his side, the almost forgotten gift from a woman he had left hanging on the wire, slowed him down just enough. They fired.

By the time Chernov brought the big .45 down to fire a second time, Hannah had gotten off a second shot and John was no longer standing. He lay on his back in the spring leaves, his hands weaving slowly above his chest.

Chernov walked to him, her sights aligned and fixated on John's face. Each step was measured and careful, feeling the ground beneath her foot before putting her whole weight on it, careful not to trip over anything. Behind her she heard Hannah ask Sharon if she was alright and then heard her move to Ellen.

Time moved slowly, as if each bit of what was happening needed to be recorded by her brain. Dim light came into the trees from the approaching dawn, somewhere deeper in the forest an owl hooted, and the man's heels rustled the leaves.

Standing over John, Chernov heard bubbling as air mixed with blood from an open wound in his chest. More blood stained his abdomen and side. John's mouth open and closed like a fish out of water. His eyes were on her face.

"Finish him," Hannah said from next to Ellen.

"No," Chernov said. She slowly lowered herself. "I want the last thing he sees is me, the last thing any of them see is me."

John, terror finally disturbing the flatness of his gaze, looked up at her. He choked, throwing blood droplets into the air. A few landed on Chernov's hands; she did not mind.

Then he was gone. Chernov jabbed two fingers into his neck, waited for a second, turned and picked up his gun, then walked over to Ellen. Hannah stood beside her, her cell phone in her hand.

"How are you doing?" she asked Ellen as she crouched down. Hannah had placed a folded t-shirt over Ellen's leg and Chernov moved Ellen's hand aside and applied pressure with her own.

"It's been a long fucking night," Ellen said. "Is Sharon all right?"

"I'm OK," Sharon said. She stood beside Hannah, hiding a little behind the tall woman's leg.

Chernov looked at Ellen then back up at Hannah, who nodded and held up a thumb with her free hand.

"You've got a gunshot wound to your upper leg," Chernov said. "Doesn't look like an artery was hit. Not too bad."

"Not too bad," Ellen said. "It hurts like hell."

Chernov grinned and turned to one side.

"Would everyone who has not been shot, blown up, or burned, please hold up your hand?"

Sharon slowly raised her hand, looking up at Hannah and then at Chernov.

"You see?"

"I was raped."

"Do you want me to ask for another show of hands? It's going to come out the same way."

"I thought of you guys when it happened, what you said, what you said to each other."

"Did it help?"

"Yes. I think so. I don't know." Ellen took a breath. "Remind them, rape kit, morning after stuff. Is he dead?"

"Very. I hit him once and I think Hannah got him twice. Damned show-off."

"Uh-rah," Hannah said softly and then returned to talking to her phone.

"He's the one who's been killing people."

"Poor choice of professions."

"No, I mean he's a serial killer. They've been looking for him. He got hired to look for you and Sharon."

"Not a mistake he'll make again. How are you feeling?"

"Couldn't be better. Wait until I tell JJ."

"Your boyfriend will have to wait."

"Not my boyfriend." Ellen took a breath and let it out slowly. "This would make a moving scene for a movie if I died about now."

"Forget the box office."

"Is he really dead?"

"Yes. He really is."

"I didn't see him die. I said I'd see him die."

"In the movie about all this, we'll make sure Bruce has his head up and sees."

"Bruce?"

"Bruce Willis. We agreed he should play you."

"He's a little old to be me. And isn't he, you know, a boy?"

"Script rewrite, not a problem – you got to go with talent."

"And he's a hell of a box office draw," Hannah said, putting a hand over the phone. "Don't forget that."

It was another seven minutes before the first Pennsylvania State Police trooper arrived and ten minutes after that before the first ambulance showed up. They kept Ellen awake until the EMTs had her on her way.

Chapter 19

Karen Deevers awoke as the sun cleared a distant tree line and saw JJ standing at the window, his back to her as he watched the dawn, his hands behind his back.

One of which held a large, automatic handgun.

"Are you going to shoot my doctor?" she asked. Her voice was soft and she doubted he could possibly have heard it but he immediately turned, as if his ears were tuned to her frequency.

In two strides the gun was gone and he held her, gently. She stroked his back. He was, she suddenly realized, crying. Karen closed her own eyes and just held him.

After a moment, he let go and brought a chair over, something complicated by his reluctance to let go of her hand.

"I've got some things to tell you," he said.

"What was the gun for?"

"That's one of the things," JJ said. "It's not the most important."

"What is?"

"I love you."

"And I love you," she said, feeling her eyes water. "Now, tell me the rest of it."

He did and then they both talked. It was enough, for the moment.

Ellen awoke later that day, which is to say just after lunch, and found Karen Deevers in a wheelchair next to her bed.

"So," Deevers asked, "what else is new?"

"Beth and Hannah got him," Ellen said.

"I know. How are you?"

"Raped, cut up, shot." Ellen paused. "Was that too dramatic?"

"Whatever you need. Be a drama queen if it helps, though I don't think it will. Never did for me."

"I think you're right. Where's Sharon?"

"Waiting for her father, her real father. Apparently, there was supposed to be some kind of joint custody but her mother had taken off with her. We found him and he's on his way down."

"Down?"

"They used to live in Chautauqua, New York. Bit of a drive, but he and his brother are coming down."

"You, you're all right?"

"No problem." She grinned. "Better than that."

"JJ...?"

"We sort of had a wake-up call. Things are moving."

"Good for you guys." Ellen looked around. "Oh, man, they must be freaking out back on the job."

"They know and they are covering the story."

"My story and I'm here." She shook her head. "I've missed everything."

"Really? Then you already know that John Theron, the self-styled 'Night Tripper,' kept a record of his kills?" She shook her head. "No one else knows and we're not releasing it until the press conference we're having at four."

"A record?"

"Not for attribution. He had a tablet. Stored photos on it. At least one for each. In the beginning, he used a point and click camera. Transferred them all to his tablet."

"Anyone who can confirm all this?"

"Nope," Karen said and watched Ellen's face fall. "On the other hand, if you see it yourself, that's your corroboration."

"It would be."

Karen pulled a tablet from a pouch on her chair. She turned it on.

"Last thing he saw on this was an article on you," she said and showed her the column. "It must have impressed him because he saved it." Then she took the tablet back.

"These pictures are not pleasant and I'm just going to show you some of them, the ones whose faces cannot be made out. You ready?"

"Yes, ma'am."

A few minutes later, Karen turned off the tablet. Tears ran down Ellen's face. One lodged on a stitch on her cheek and stayed there, catching the light like a small gem.

"A bunch of the other pictures are worse," she said.

"Could have been me," Ellen said. "And the others."

"Wasn't. Now, I guess you have to tell some of the story for the women for whom it was."

"I think I do."

JJ stood in the hall outside Ellen's room, his phone pressed against his ear. "Hello," a woman said.

"It's JJ," he said. "Been trying to get you. Have you heard the news yet?"

"What news?"

"They got him, early this morning. He was shot dead by some women he was getting ready to murder."

Aretha Taylor cried and JJ waited. She did not break the connection, as if he loaned her strength through the electrons, and he did not break the connection because it was all he could do for a friend.

Elizabeth Chernov, still wearing her Army jacket, watched the man be led by the State Trooper. His name, she had been told, was Peter Derego. He and his brother had driven down from New York.

He was Sherrie Stuart's father.

The police told Chernov he was coming and he and his daughter would be in the area for several days as some loose ends were resolved. The first loose end, of course, was Sherrie.

Under the supervision of the Child Services representative, Chernov had stayed with the little girl who had not known her father was still alive. So now Sherrie stood beside Chernov, holding her hand, watching a man she had not seen for more than three years approach.

Derego had tears in his eyes as soon as they turned up the walk and he saw Sharon. For her part, the little girl squeezed Chernov's fingers tighter and tighter before finally looking up at the woman. Chernov looked down.

"It's all right," Chernov said, smiling. "Like I said, I'm easy to find. You can always call."

Sharon looked back at her father and Chernov felt the girl's fingers loosen and, with all the strength she had learned in her life, she willed her hand not to tighten, to relax its grip, and to let her run to her father.

Chernov watched the two embrace and cry and laugh and all the other things a child and parent who love one another do when coming together. She stood there, smiling, Hannah O'Bannon standing a few steps behind her.

Finally, Peter Derego, his little girl in his arms, walked up to her. Sherrie hung onto him like a drowning person, her face buried into his shoulder.

"Thank you," he said. "They told me you saved her."

"It wasn't that much," Chernov said. She patted Sharon's back and saw Derego turn slightly, moving the girl away from her hand.

"It was everything," Derego said. "Everything."

"She has my number. I thought…"

"That was very nice of you," Derego said. "But maybe she should put this behind her for a while."

"Of course."

"You were in the Army?"

"Yes."

"Thank you for your service," Derego said. He smiled and turned away and walked back to his car. Sharon looked up from his shoulder and smiled. Chernov knew she would remember that image forever as she smiled back like this was just an ordinary day and her heart wasn't slowly tearing in two.

She watched as they got back into the car and drove away to the motel they would stay at and begin to build their lives together. It was only after they were out of sight, after the last wave from Sharon, that she cried.

Hannah held her and said nothing. But she held her friend as long as it was needed. Sometimes there are no words.

Three months later, Chernov was called by Peter Derego. He gave her the date of Sharon's birthday, which was just coming up, and requested that she call his daughter.

"I think she's got some roots here now," he said. "But she thinks of you as her older sister. So, if it wouldn't be a bother…?"

Chernov told him it wouldn't be and she would be happy to talk to Sharon. She was.

Three days after the reunion of Sharon Stuart with her father, the body of Donald Brunner, lately a sergeant in the New Joyton Police Department, was found on the banks of the Brandywine River. The medical examiner ruled he had died from a shotgun blast to the chest approximately 72 hours before the body was found.

It was two months before the body of a Mr. Thomas Tallman was found in a shallow grave beside an abandoned barn. Though the body was significantly decomposed, the medical examiner ruled that Mr. Tallman, late of the methamphetamine business, most probably had died from gunshot wounds; more specifically, two to the head.

The Reverend Donaldson was arrested the same day as Karen Deevers asked about her husband and his pistol. An anonymous call came in to the Chester County Sheriff's Office suggesting they go to the Aryan Nation compound, home of the Church of Jesus Christ-Christian, and see if they could find some people of interest. Apparently, the caller was unaware that the most interesting person, Ellen Parker, had been there and also was unaware Donaldson's guest, John "Night Tripper" Theron, was dead.

The deputies arrived before the reverend, noted the open gate with its lock and chain lying on the ground, and decided they had probable cause to enter. After all, there might be a crime in progress and they really wanted to protect the rights and property of some asshole Nazis who had moved into their county.

The Reverend Donaldson arrived shortly after they found John's back room and the trail of blood drops that led to the chain link fence with blood-smeared razor wire. As they examined the fence, they met fellow officers with a search dog following the trail up the hill from the shooting site.

The search dog was brought into the compound and alerted to the reverend's office. It turned out there were several hiding places in the floor. The dog did better than Doctor John and found two hideaways containing large quantities of methamphetamine, product Reverend Donaldson was supposed to assist in delivering to customers of Mr. Tallman.

As he was led away in handcuffs, Donaldson complained about his fortune, saying that he should have realized his congregation had been infiltrated by DEA agents when the number of people who regularly tithed increased. However, there had been no infiltration; his remark was a measure of his loss of faith.

The man known as Chris continued as a CI – Confidential Informant – for the Pennsylvania State Police's task force on the drug trade. With the abrupt departure of Mr. Tallman, he was uncertain as to his future. But Mr. Books, newly installed as the chief executive officer of their enterprise, assured him nothing had changed.

It seemed the new boss was a lot like the old boss.

160

Ellen Parker was nominated for a Pulitzer for her story of John Theron, the Night Tripper, but, as before, she did not win.

She had nightmares and a startle reaction. Hannah O'Bannon and Beth Chernov encouraged her to see a therapist. Ellen was a little reluctant until they pointed out they had access to firearms and Ellen agreed to go.

So did they, just to be sure.

Ellen's startle and nightmares went away, though she remained pretty aware of what was going on around her. But then, her grandfather had once observed she had been alert as a young girl, and he knew about such things.

The three women formed what they privately referred to as the "Shot to Hell Club" and meet twice a month for lunch and more often just to hang out – sometimes you get lucky and find friends in the damnedest circumstances.

A fourth member joined their group as the summer ended, but that's another story.

Steven M. Silver

Excerpt from *Hidden Things*, the fourth Ellen Parker novel.

Chapter 1: Day One

The road the police officer rode went down a corn stalk corridor holding onto the August heat and humidity of eastern Pennsylvania. Above, dark clouds promised some kind of cooling rain. He glanced up through aviator sunglasses and wondered if the rain would, in fact, bring any cooling before it left – Pennsylvania, he knew, was an inveterate liar about its own weather.

He passed the marker for the Coalville borough limits but did not slow down; it was easier to turn his Ford Expedition around at the T-intersection a half mile ahead than wrestling the big SUV on the narrow road. That is why he saw the car with New York plates.

It was across and slightly down the crossing road as he stopped at the intersection. He turned and pulled in behind it, keeping the Expedition's right-hand wheels on pavement and angling its nose toward the road. The shoulder was narrow before giving way to a drainage ditch bordered by an old but still upright barbed wire fence.

The car was a recent and big Toyota SUV in white. He grinned; at least it wasn't in that silver that all Toyotas seemed to come in. Apparently, they did have another color. It was barely off the road. He could see no one in it as he called its plate number into the dispatcher, feeling, not for the first time that day, a touch of irritation that his computer was still down. While waiting for his request for vehicle registration information, he flipped his flashers on. The officer picked up his dark blue cap from the seat and stepped out of the Ford.

He was a tall black man who had gotten into the habit, courtesy of the Pennsylvania Army National Guard and three tours in the sandbox, of shaving his head, though he permitted himself a carefully trimmed moustache. His clear brown eyes did nothing to hide the intelligence using them. His blue uniform shirt was short sleeved and revealed muscled arms his wife still insisted on describing, after twenty years, as "all business." On his chest, across from his silver Coalville police badge, a thin silver nametag bore the name "Peterson" and his collar tabs had small, silver sergeant chevrons.

It still looked like rain. A white man approached, walking across the field, burdened by a bag hanging over a shoulder and holding a camera. The dispatcher called back with no warrants or wants on the vehicle or its registered owner, a Robert Blasingame.

162

"I didn't get far enough off the road?" the man asked, pausing at the fence. He had sandy hair cut short and well, about two inches over six feet in height, weight around 190, though his shoulders beneath an old plaid felt shirt suggested he might be closer to 200, blue jeans, and ankle-high gray hiking shoes. He had smile lines and pale blue eyes that drooped at the ends, a curious combination of humor and sadness coexisting on his face.

"You're good," Peterson said. He stepped across the ditch. "May I see your license, sir?"

"Sure," Blasingame said. He opened his bag and put his camera into it and then produced his wallet. He handed over his license. It had a better than average picture of him and his name.

"Thank you, Mister Blasingame," Peterson said. He handed the license back. "What were you taking pictures of, the crash site?"

"Not really," Blasingame said. He looked back across the field. "I'm an amateur photographer and I wanted to try to get some shots of the plant life coming back." He pointed. "The burned area goes into the trees bordering the field and you can see where bushes and things got crushed by the impact." He turned back to the officer and smiled slightly. "It's the contrast that I was trying for, the flattened stuff and the new sprouts, the black area and the new green. Not some kind of ghoul, just like to take pictures of nature. For a photography class I'm taking."

"What kind of camera are you using?"

Blasingame opened the lid of the bag and took out a black camera.

"It's a Canon EOS. I really need to take a class in operating it. The thing is smarter than I am." He grinned.

He said it with the kind of self-deprecating tone men use when they don't want to brag but are probably pretty proficient at whatever skill they are talking about. Peterson nodded.

"Can I see some of your work?"

"Sure." Blasingame took a second to bring the display to life and then he handed the camera to Peterson. "That's the last shot. You can scroll back by... You got it. Probably know more about these things than I do."

"Not likely," Peterson said as he looked at the pictures. "My car's computer has taken a personal affront to me and I haven't been able to get anything but a big blue error message all shift. I'd shoot the damned thing but then there would be all that paperwork."

Blasingame chuckled and then tilted his neck to see the screen.

"I think that's the best of them."

"It is a good shot," Peterson said, nodding. "You have an eye for photos."

"Thanks." He turned and looked back at the burned field.

"I don't really know much about what happened, just caught it on the news last month."

"Yeah, the fire spread fast," Peterson said. There were no more pictures to see and he handed the camera back to Blasingame. "It was pretty dry and had been for a while. Our fire people had their hands full beating it down."

"The news talked a lot about the townspeople pitching in," Blasingame said as he put the camera in its bag and checked the lid's latches. He rested his hands on the top wire. "Volunteers."

"Small town, everyone knows everyone; trouble comes, people pitch in to help. We're not like the bigger towns like Downingtown south of here where you only know the people living next door."

"Were you here?"

"Not immediately," Peterson said. "I'd just gotten off night shift when I got the recall. By the time I arrived, you had the whole fire department here. They came through a gate over there," he pointed down the road, "and were working on both the wreck and the trees."

"Were the volunteers already here?"

"Most of them," Peterson said, "though people kept arriving all through the morning." He shook his head. "Bad stuff. The place was a mess. The plane actually hit at first in the field beyond the gate, kind of bounced through the fence over there and tumbled. The fire, well, you can see where it really flared up. That was the forward portions of the plane, where the engines came to rest." He shook his head again. "Bad stuff. All thirty-two people died in the crash."

"Twenty-seven in the crash," Blasingame said. "Five on the way to or in the hospital."

You don't know much about it but you know where they all died.

Peterson nodded, saying nothing, but a small alarm bell went off in the part of his brain that was Coalville Township Police Department blue.

"Well, Mister Blasingame," he said, "this is private land and…"

"I understand," Blasingame said. He took off his bag and reached over the fence to put it on the ground but the officer held out his hand. Blasingame grinned. "Thanks."

Blasingame put both hands on the top of the post and, with little seeming effort, vaulted over the fence. Peterson handed him the bag.

"Thanks again, sergeant," Blasingame said, slipping the strap over his shoulder.

"No problem," Peterson said. "Where are you headed?"

"Here, actually. On vacation. I want to spend some time taking pictures of barns and covered bridges, and I really want to see some of the antique stores. Thought I'd slip over to Lancaster County for the Amish farms."

"Good place for it," Peterson said. "Just don't take pictures of the Amish themselves. They dislike it."

"Gotcha."

"Staying at the motel?"

"No, I've got reservations at the Willow Run Bed and Breakfast. Have you heard anything about it?"

"I'm told it's pretty good," Peterson said. "Newer place, been in business just a few years. Nice ladies run it. It's just a mile west of here."

"My first time here. And my first vacation in a couple of years." He smiled again. "Motels seem too much like business, you know? So I figured a B and B would be nicer."

"They seem to be making a go of it," Peterson said. "Near Willow Run, you have a couple of fast food places but, if you go looking for dinner, there's a nice restaurant right in the center of town. Alfredo's. And a diner next to the township buildings, it's pretty good." He smiled slightly. "It's where most of the police go."

"Thanks for the information," Blasingame said. He held out his hand. "Be safe, sergeant."

"Thanks," Peterson said, shaking his hand. "I'll wait until you've pulled out."

Peterson waited in his car, its blue and reds flashing, as Blasingame drove onto the road and then turned around at the gate. As he came back, Peterson raised his hand to Blasingame's wave. Then he picked up his microphone.

"Dispatch, Peterson. Run a check for me on a Robert L. Blasingame, address on his vehicle registration that you just ran."

Copy, Sergeant Peterson.

The alarm bell was still insisting, though very gently, that attention be paid to it.

Ellen Parker drove her Honda CR-V through Coalville, a journey that took relatively little time as the town was small, almost tiny. Well, it was, at least in comparison, if you worked in Philadelphia.

She silently offered the town an apology. Back in Ohio, where she grew up, small towns were the rule – getting down to Cincinnati was a big deal.

Now here I am, all jaded, so much so that I use words like 'jaded.'

She smiled, something she did easily. A thin woman, what in southern Ohio might have been called "rawboned" with only slight exaggeration, her high cheekbones and sharp nose were softened by brown eyes that looked around her with openness.

Ellen slowed down at a pedestrian crossing in the middle of a block as a woman and child stepped onto it. The woman looked in her direction and nodded as Ellen stopped. Ellen looked around while she waited.

Coalville was dominated by one- and two-story buildings. All seemed in good shape with none needing paint. Bright banners hung from lampposts; some said "PA's heart!" while others "Welcome Home!"

The crosswalk clear, she let her car roll forward. The Garmin told her to look for an upcoming right hand turn off of Stanford Avenue, which the county road bringing her into town had magically turned into. She came up on the cross street and made her right. Very quickly, she was out of town and surrounded by country. Small town, indeed.

Five minutes later, the Garmin insisted she was at her destination, which appeared to be a single, gravel-covered lane. She turned onto it and ignored the Garmin's insistence she turn around. The lane took her through some trees and then, when the county road behind her disappeared, she arrived at a paved parking lot and scattered buildings, all dominated by a two-story log cabin.

A carved sign out front said, "Willow Run B&B". She smiled and stretched before opening the door.

Now her vacation officially started.

Ellen swung the car door wide and stepped out of the car. While the parking lot pavement reflected the heat, the woods were close to the buildings, almost cradling them, and she looked forward to walking through the trees.

"Are you Ellen Parker?" a woman's voice called from within the log cabin.

"I am," she said. "I'm early." She looked but could see no one behind the screen door.

"Not a problem," the woman said. "Come on in."

Ellen walked into the cabin and found herself in a broad room with heavily padded chairs and couches. To the left a closed door stood beside a staircase that disappeared above. Paintings of wildlife competed with photographs of country scenes – both appeared to be done by good artists – and both covered the walls above waist-high bookshelves. The shelves were full of paperbacks and hardbound books. Board games piled on a shelf threatened to collapse into themselves and Ellen wondered how Monopoly and Scrabble would merge. Maybe spell your way out of jail?

To the right, the room opened on a dining area almost as large. Small tables with pairs of chairs stood against the walls while a long table, big enough to encourage wondering how it had managed to be brought in, took up the middle with a dozen chairs, only three of which matched.

"Back in here," the voice said from beyond the dining room and Ellen walked further into the house.

She found the woman in the kitchen putting away blue dishes. While the kitchen had a well-lit island, it seemed, after the first two rooms, surprisingly small.

The woman was tall and broad shouldered with a white person's complexion reflecting a fair amount of time spent outdoors. Ellen recognized her from the web site where she made her reservations; her name was Patti Taylor and she was, the site said, "Primary Cook, kitchen Czarina, and struggling Gardner." Though in her mid-40s, something she did not attempt to camouflage, she looked like athletics were still a part of her life.

"Pour yourself some coffee," Patti said. "Behind you, it's set up for use any time."

Ellen turned and found a coffee urn with a bunch of cups, all different, all handmade, spread across a broad shelf above it. She poured herself a cup.

"Cream, real thing, in the fridge," Pattie said taking bowls from the dishwasher.

"Prefer it straight," Ellen said. "Can I pour you one?"

"Thanks," Patti said, "but I'm still working on one somewhere around here. Switch to tea for dinner." She looked up. "You read all the stuff on the site?"

"Pretty much," Ellen said.

Patti faced her, a smile appearing as she found her coffee cup. She took a sip.

"Breakfast starts at seven, done by nine, in the evening we put out cheese, wine, fruit, that sort of thing. Food bars and fruit always in the fridge, use them any time. Books, borrow whatever you like, drop off any of your own you don't want to carry home."

"Who's your photographer?"

"Like those? They're by our guests. We had several birders who took a zillion pictures and sent some back to us. And the deer ones, they're by a professional fella whose stuff is in Sports Illustrated. He got tired of taking pictures of concussions, I guess. He's in Australia now, documenting what they're doing after their wildfires."

"They're pretty good."

"You a photographer?"

"No," Ellen said. "I've worked with some and I like to get outdoors."

"You know from our site that we're surrounded by trees. State game land just to the west, county park to the south, numerous trails all round, there's a map in your room. Please use it because we try not to give the search and rescue people any more business than we have to."

Ellen nodded.

"You're here for the week," Patti said. "So we have you in the furthest cabin from here, which we call the 'main house' because we are bereft of imagination. We have a fellow from New York staying a week and a couple of guys staying a week, but everyone else is one- or two-night people. One family coming in tonight. Lots of kids. Regulars, this is their third visit. They'll be upstairs here in the main house. Shouldn't be too rowdy."

"I'll try not to be myself."

"Too bad. Anyway, Joyce will do breakfast tomorrow morning. Watch out for her; her goal in life is to make a piece of French toast large enough to sink a good-sized container ship."

"I think I'm in love."

"Sorry, she's taken. We've got WI-FI via cable; cellphone service here can be spotty. Landline phone here in the kitchen with our number and all the usual emergency numbers on the posted sheet beside it. We live back up the lane near the entrance and can get here pretty quick if you need us."

"Laundry? The site didn't say."

"Carefully guarded secret. Utility room out the back door, beyond the dining room, on the right. If you use it, wait until after everyone in the main house has done their morning showers as it draws on the same hot water tank. Not a problem if you are using just cold water. Early afternoon is usually safe. If you are in a rush, there's a coin-op in town, just as you enter from here.

Look to the right, right after the golden arches but before the Wise Owl book store."

"Thanks." Ellen paused. "Anything besides deer in the woods?"

"Occasional dragons, that sort of thing," Patti said, "but not this time of year."

"Already migrated east, then, have they?"

"Pretty much. We have coyotes, you'll probably never see them."

"Why not?"

"Maybe a Navy SEAL, bless their black hearts, could get close enough, but most people are too noisy in the trees. Skunks, raccoons, you want to keep your distance because of the possibility of rabies. County has stopped counting rabid animals. If they approach you, that's usually a pretty good signal to back off."

"All right."

"Anything else I can tell you? I'll make things up if I don't know the answer."

"Sounds like some of the people I've interviewed. No, no other questions."

"Let's get your key and let me show you your cabin."

The cabin was larger than Ellen expected. Two queen-sized beds, covered by quilted blankets, dominated the pine-paneled room but it had a pair of well-padded chairs facing a wide picture window. A solid table with a firmer chair was against a wall with a small card describing the log-on procedures for the WI-FI connection. A chest of drawers bordered a wall. A large bathroom was in the back.

"Very nice," she said and Patti grinned.

"Be sure to leave your porch light on," Patti said. "You're facing away from the main house and night around here gets very dark."

"That's all right," Ellen said. "I kind of like the night."

"Some people do."

"I think we'll take that service plaza," the driver of the dark blue Chevy Suburban said as the green sign with white lettering came into view; the sun was going down behind it and it was hard to see clearly in spite of his sunglasses. He was white and in his late forties. He wore his hair short along his temples that partially hid his scattering of gray hair and made him look like he had been a soldier at some time, an occupation he had never tried. Like the man next to him, he wore a sport coat. Both men wore tinted aviator-style sunglasses but only the driver sported a tie. People who knew of him, and there were very few who did, just knew him as Radisson, no first name. Only a very few knew his first name was Daniel, only one person on Earth was allowed to call him Danny, and that person sat next to him. "How far to our exit?"

"Morgantown exit is about eight miles from here, six from the service center. There should be a motel right after the exit. Or we can press on to Coalville."

"I want to come on it in the morning. Did you do that math in your head?" He liked to tease his partner.

His partner was a few years younger, more athletic appearing, and wore his hair short in imitation of Radisson, though his was obviously a reddish blond. His name was Michael Bornstein. People who knew him had, when he was much younger, called him Mikey. Since he had teamed up with Radisson, anyone who knew him just called him by his last name. The two men had been lovers for four years.

"Had to use my fingers. Quick trip from Allentown. Less than an hour."

"We spent that long trying to get our lunch there. Worst airport I've ever flown into."

"Did you hear what Graber said about it?"

"That it sucked?"

"He's a pilot, he ought to know. On the other hand, using our own plane made it easier to get our stuff in and out past security."

"He used to be a smuggler. Goes back to the cowboy days. Knows all the tricks."

"I think I could teach him a couple."

"Don't pick on the straight people, Michael. It's cruel."

"Car guys were on top of things, though."

"Always nice to use a car with local plates. I don't like standing out."

"Have you seen this boat?"

"Which one?"

"The one by Hinckley. This one." He held up the magazine from his lap and Radisson took a quick look. "Matt Lauer has one."

"Yeah, the *Picnic*. Very nice."

"They do good work, but it's pricey."

"Well, yeah, Matt Lauer. Television guy, he's got to have a fortune."

"But we can dream."

"Always. I don't suppose Mr. Fredericks' friend down in Florida handles Hinckleys."

"Already checked the brochure. Afraid not."

"I like the Whaler 360 more, anyway."

"You just like three outboards."

"I am an outboard man, no question. You want to call Mr. Books, let him know we're about to enter his territory? Tell him where we're going to spend the night, so he understands we're not pressing in without telling him."

"Always pays to be courteous. I'll call his guy when we stop at the plaza."

"And let Mr. Fredericks know we tipped our hat politely to Mr. Books. He'll want to know that we didn't forget."

"All in the nature of political politeness."

Radisson chuckled as he hit his turn signal.

"Mr. Books probably is worried," he said as he negotiated the ramp into the plaza, "that we're going to start shooting up the place like Wyatt Earp, being from New York and all."

"We're not?" Bornstein took off his sunglasses and revealed gray-blue eyes. "You never let me have any fun."

"Keep thinking about that 360," Radisson said, grinning at the other man's joke and revealing smile lines deeply creasing his face. "We'll have a hell of a lot of fun with that."

"Not only with that," the other man said, stroking the inside of Radisson's thigh as they pulled into a parking place. He smiled and opened the door. "Got to make my call," he said and stepped out.

"Teaser," Radisson said. "I'm going to hit the rest room. You want a soda?"

"No cruising," the other man said, raising his smart phone and studying the screen. "Yes, please, whatever diet they have."

"Got it." He turned to go.

"You're snagged," Bornstein said, his voice low, and Radisson stopped.

Keeping his back to his car door, Radisson felt behind him and freed his coat from the handgun he carried. The Suburban was tall and the door was a good shield.

"Thanks," he said. He adjusted his coat. "All right now?"

"You're fine."

"Didn't even think to check," Radisson said. He shook his head. "Good thing we're retiring."

"Hey, on the road all day. Get tired, distracted."

"No excuse," Radisson said, his voice firm. "Be right back."

Bornstein watched him go and then punched a number into his phone. There was no question that Radisson was a professional, but sometimes he was too hard on himself. No slack at all.

Of course, in their business, which had nothing to do with fishing boats and everything to do with the Glocks both men carried, slack was for amateurs.

Woman on the Wire cover by Eric Strehl
Blackheart Studios, http://www.ejstrehl.com

Also by Steven M. Silver

With Susan Rogers, Ph.D. *Light in the heart of darkness: EMDR and the treatment of war and terrorism survivors.*

Poetry

American Travelers
Hot Chrome, Smooth Leather, and a Red Bandanna
Victor Echo Zero Five

Fiction

The Wild Geese Saga
Mercenary's Heart
Mercenary's Honor
Mercenary's Code
Mercenary's Logic
Mercenary's Destiny
Mercenary's Soldiers
Mercenary's Redemption
Mercenary's Courage
Mercenary's Peace
Mercenary's Justice
Mercenary's Humanity
Mercenary's Promise

The Ellen Parker Series
A Dangerous Man
Killers
Woman on the Wire
Hidden Things
Child in the Dark

173

www.ingramcontent.com/pod-product-compliance
Lightning Source LLC
Chambersburg PA
CBHW060646260626
47161CB00008B/3022